Haunted Houses

Haunted Houses

Lynne Tillman

Red Lemonade

a Cursor publishing community

Brooklyn, New York

2011

Library of Congress Cataloging-in-Publication Data

Tillman, Lynne.

Haunted houses / by Lynne Tillman
p   .cm.
ISBN 978-1-935869-09-2
I. Title
PS3570.I42 H3 1987
813/.54 19
                    86-25156

Cover design by Charles Orr
Interior design by Fogelson + Lubliner

Red Lemonade
a Cursor publishing community
Brooklyn, New York

http://redlemona.de

Table of Contents

1   Part I
49   Part II
83   Part III
115   Part IV
157   Part V

To Iris Tillman Hill

We are all haunted houses.
—H. D., in *Tribute to Freud*

Part I

Chapter 1

Her father liked to scare her. He knew she adored him. He'd creep into her room early in the morning or late at night and jump on her and she'd cry. He'd console her with kisses and hugs. Years later Jane would say, It's a hard habit to break. Loving madmen. Jane's parents, particularly her father, had wanted a son, having two girls already, and had waited nearly seven years before making the unsuccessful attempt to have him. Jane's mother would need an operation after Jane's birth, which would put an end once and for all to her child bearing days, but Jane was innocent of this fact, as well as their desire for a son. Otherwise she was not a difficult birth.

At two she had tried to claim her father as her own, covering his face with her little body, and shouting, He's my daddy, my daddy, to her much older sisters, who could dismiss that kind of behavior as babyish. But Jane was driven. She became Daddy's girl to the chagrin of her mother, who had her hands full anyway. The third child is always the easiest, she heard her mother say to a woman who was visiting. It's like she's raising herself.

Jane's first boyfriend, when she was three, was a morose, skinny kid who lived on the floor below, his whole family skinny and very pale. After a pretend marriage that lasted a year, they were separated because her family moved away to the suburbs, and she asked one of her sisters if this meant they were divorced. Yes, she answered, and Jane promptly found a second boyfriend, Jimmy, who lived on the next block. He, too, was a peculiar boy, three years older than Jane, and elusive; she could never tell if he liked her or not. Jane couldn't figure out who her parents liked either, though her father said he liked everybody. In any case he was nice to everybody and they didn't see him when he was sulking in the basement because he couldn't hook up the speaker to the radio. He put a telephone down there, ostensibly to call his mother, who didn't get along with Jane's mother, and he called her every day.

When she played with Jimmy, Jane insisted upon wearing dresses. He's too wild, her mother told her. But his nostrils flare when he speaks, she responded, which meant to Jane that Jimmy was sensitive, like a rabbit. She could even tell him about the children's book she loved and hated because it confused her. There was a little girl who had a blanket. The blanket got a hole in it. She wanted to get rid of the hole so she decided to cut it out. She cut it out and the hole got bigger. She cut that out too, and the hole got bigger. Eventually the hole disappeared but so did the blanket. The little girl cried and Jane was genuinely puzzled.

An unspoken contract existed between Jane and her father; she went along to ball games and amusement parks when other fathers brought their sons. She played seriously with their sons, stretching across the slippery iron horse, reaching for the brass ring, though she was afraid of heights, reaching for it as if she really cared about winning. She hated losing her balance. Jane was almost certain that her father was her partner in this charade, and that he knew she was humoring him. But his moods changed as fast as she changed

TV channels. He'd always been violent and had used his belt on Jane when she was small, but these violations were more than balanced by his good looks and charm. Her violations were almost invisible, something about the way she answered a question, something about the way she walked into a room. Everyone was in love with her father, Jane thought. He was so young-looking that her oldest sister's friends thought he looked more like her sister's date than her father.

He liked to read to his daughters. And he, more often than her mother, put Jane to bed at night. Occasionally he recited Churchill's memorable speech about blood, sweat, and tears, or read the Gettysburg Address, or cited the George Medal, which George VI had instituted for commoners, like her and him, to commend them for "obscure heroism in squalid places." But while he had read Shakespeare to her sisters, he chose for her Lord Chesterfield's *Letters to his Son*. Lord Chesterfield wrote many long and logical letters to his profligate son, who should have been in England, not France, of the great harm that would come to him should he continue gambling and whoring. These letters, like Churchill's speech, were supposed to comfort Jane, who had trouble sleeping at night, but as she was only eight when Chesterfield was read to her, she was not yet thinking of leaving home, or gambling, or whoring, or of being a whore, and unlike Chesterfield's son, she barely even had an allowance. These letters were harbingers of some future time and didn't comfort her. At their best they did put her to sleep. Jane never told her father not to read these letters to her. He might sulk or go into a rage. She became an Anglophile anyway.

Watching her oldest sister's boyfriends come and go, Jane acted like a lady-in-waiting to her—getting her brush, finding her bag, studying her image in the mirror. When her sister put on makeup, it looked to Jane as if she were preparing for a part in a play. There was a solemnness pervading the bathroom, mixed in with smells from the older girl's lipstick and powder and perfume with which she anointed herself. Glowing with artifice and anxiety, Jane's sister walked down the stairs, viewed by Jane at the top, lying flat on her stomach so that the boyfriend might not see. Then they disappeared, her sister and her date, both actors in another world.

By the time Jimmy announced that he loved her, or rather her shadow, which she knew meant her, the fact that they were in different grades meant more to her than having won the attenuated battle for his affections. He was eleven and not as skinny as he'd once been, and even though his nostrils still quivered, he just wasn't as cute, she thought, so she pretended not to understand what he was saying, which was, she discovered early, a disguise that worked.

Besides, she had fallen in love with Michael, another bad boy from good people who couldn't control him, or that's what Jane's mother said. She usually added, He'll grow out of it, as if his character were a pair of pants. With Jane, Michael stole useless things from Woolworth's. She stole the tops of Dixie cups for him and watched with pleasure—a small smile on an otherwise impassive face—when Michael ripped birthday party decorations off basement walls. Jane never gave parties and hated basements, where they were always held. Her family's basement was used by her mother to do the laundry, her middle sister, to practice ballet, and by her father, less specifically. It had a ballet barre, a Ping-Pong table, and bookshelves in which her father kept paperbacks like *How to Live with Your Anxiety* and hardcovers about Winston Churchill and Abraham Lincoln. One

Lincoln book had a picture of all the accomplices to his assassination, hanging on the gallows. Five wore trousers, and one, a dress. Their heads were covered with white bags. She stared at the image for long periods of time in the almost empty recreation room, the room itself weird a joke to Jane, whose sense of humor was grim. Watching the conclusion of *A Farewell to Arms* on television with her mother, she said, flatly, He should get an erector set. Her mother laughed, despite herself, said nothing, and worried about Jane's strange ideas.

As Jane grew up her father's alarm at what he called her wild ways also grew. The way she washed dishes. The way she flipped electric switches. It was all wild. Her parents fought over her too. During one fight Jane's mother took all Jane's father's clothes and threw them on the floor. Jane observed the action from her place at the top of the stairs, this time not lying flat on her stomach but seated as if in the balcony of the U.N. At school Jane was considered something of a diplomat, but not by her father, who didn't move out as her mother said she wanted him to do. Jane wrote in her diary: Now that I've seen this, life is different. Life is not that different, she discovered, when Jimmy reappeared with another neighborhood girl and Jane thought she was in love with him all over again. She thought that showed maturity—to be able to be in love with someone for so long.

Innocent kissing ended in the seventh grade and Jane and Michael broke up. They had reached the age when kisses and hugs were no longer sufficient. Sex filtered through the classroom and gym in a form as regimented as grade school education. Jane drew back. She didn't want to be like other girls. She wanted to be respected. Respect and sex were as far from one another as she was from being an adult, a state she wanted to reach quickly, so that she would know things and be free, and not care about what people thought.

When she reached her adolescence, having grown into it with breasts Jane thought of as bumps, her sisters' male friends took notice of her. It was the summer she turned thirteen and one sister bought her stockings and Arpège perfume. Jane lived in white shorts and a red boat neck. Her sisters' friends came out on weekends. One young man, an Austrian, looked at her in a way that made her uncomfortable. Considering himself a genius, as well as a good judge of women, he told her sister that Jane was a regular Lolita. Jane was reading a novel called *The Violated*, whose central character, Sheila, was a girl her age. Sheila was directing *Hamlet*; it was in the middle of the book. Sheila announced to the neighborhood kids who were the cast, Everyone talks dirty to Ophelia.

Her father said Jimmy was dirty. He didn't brush his teeth much, even when he dropped by to see Jane. Sometimes their meetings were accidental, but Jane didn't really believe in accidents. If questioned she would deride notions of fate—she was very rational—but still she thought Jimmy and she were meant for each other. Now that he was a senior, he drove his convertible into the city, and spent time with people Jane didn't know. Though one high school yearbook picture shows her sitting in his convertible, it was unusual to find her there.

Of the people Jane knew when she was fourteen, it was Lois who seemed like her only real friend. Lois wanted to go to Hollywood, to be an actress. She wore falsies that stuck out from her narrow chest like small ice-cream cones. I don't care who puts his hand where, she laughed raucously. The two walked around town singing and cracking jokes. They danced in front of clothes stores and beauty parlors.

To Jane, Lois was revolutionary because she just wanted to have a good time. It was raining as they walked along Main Street. Jane told Lois that the first time she ever took a shower she made her father go in with her because she was afraid of the water. So she told Lois, who was laughing, I insisted we use an umbrella and we stood there, my father and me, under that open umbrella. Your father doesn't sound that bad, Lois said, thinking that Jane might have exaggerated about his temper. You'll see, Jane answered.

Her sisters were hardly ever home, and Jane had her parents to herself. She couldn't decide if her father was much crazier than he used to be, or whether, now that she was alone, she noticed it more. It didn't help that business was starting to fall off. His younger brother Larry, who was also his business partner, never seemed to worry. He was divorced, ran around with women, played the horses, and saw a psychiatrist. To Jane, Uncle Larry had style, but he wasn't a favorite of her mother's. Years later someone told Jane that her mother was always too much in love with her father. Jane had never considered that what her mother was in was love.

With some determination Jane asked Lois home. Like everyone else Lois found Jane's father handsome and charming. All the women loved dancing with him, the men thought he dyed his hair. Jane told Lois, in the bathroom where her two older sisters had once gotten ready for dates, that when she was five she used to hide from him here because the door had a lock. They were practicing smoking. They put on go-go pink lipstick and black mascara and left the bathroom. Jane's father was in the hall, Jane knew the look. His face contorted as he yelled, his hand touching his belt. It was about her makeup. He pushed Jane out of the house, told her that she shouldn't come back, and slammed the door. Lois and Jane walked along in silence for a while, then Jane said, I'm used to it.

When summer came Lois got a job as an acting counselor in a camp, and Jane's father insisted she work for him in his office near Times Square. Every morning they caught the 7:52 with the men and their sons. Boys who had been seniors when she was a freshman sat in suits and ties, beefier and older, holding *The New York Times* in front of their no-longer-boyish faces. Jane got the print all over her hands and never mastered the technique of folding the paper so that she didn't stick her arm in her father's face. They got out at Penn Station and walked to work, where she had nothing to do. Her father invented work for her. She typed letters with samples and sent them to businesses chosen from the telephone book. She was as friendly as a dog to any customer who walked in. She watched her father. Uncle Larry rarely came into the office but when he did, her father cheered up. Larry was always optimistic and then off to the racetrack. He loved the horses.

It was a hot summer, and on a particularly hot morning her father suggested she go to a movie on Forty-second Street. It was about 10 A.M. and Jane asked the woman in the box office if it was all right to go in. The woman said, You just pay your money and you go in, which Jane could figure out for herself, having paid her money and gone in to many movie houses. She took a seat near the aisle and the attendant looked up her dress, bending down, being very obvious. She moved to a middle seat and a young man in a light tan cap sat down next to her. The place was empty. She moved; he moved. She couldn't go back to work so soon. She moved again, he moved again. He placed his hand on her knee and Jane looked at it. It lay there for a while. Jane wondered if he thought he was Holden Caulfield, with that cap on. She kept looking at his hand. It was dark and she could have done anything and no one would have seen or known. She felt something, and it wasn't exactly that she felt sorry for him. His hand moved a little and feeling that she didn't care what happened she got up and walked out. Jane wandered around Times Square, settling on playing Fascination till enough time had passed and she could return to her father. Two Doris Day reruns, she heard herself telling him. You know, they're always the same.

Lois said she wanted to go to UCLA to study acting, and then try to get roles as a comedian or a character actress. I'm not that pretty, she stated indifferently, I couldn't be the romantic type, but somebody has to be Rosalind Russell. Jane didn't know what she wanted to do. None of Lois's friends were as determined as she was. One of them called Jane on a Sunday morning and told her to sit down. It was very early. Jane said what's wrong and the friend said Lois is dead. She was killed in a car crash.

A funeral for a sixteen-year-old is awful. Lois's friends weren't allowed to go to the cemetery. All of them stood together in one part of the chapel, far from the family, so as not to remind them of their loss. Jane's parents respected her silence and didn't fight with each other that day. Jane saw Lois everywhere, when she took a bath, when she turned off the lights. There was a glow that she decided was Lois. Without knowing it she mourned her death for nearly eight months until spring came and a boy from another school made her laugh about death. She felt she was betraying Lois in one way, and in another way she knew Lois would understand. There was something horribly funny about death. For Lois's sake Jane pledged to change her life, to become different so that her death wouldn't seem so stupid. Jane had always wanted to live her life differently.

The same guys who'd been her friends in grade school were now hanging out in the halls and smoking dope or taking advantage of girls, and Jane might wave or say hello to Michael but that was all. Her childhood was definitely over, she thought, each time she saw how far apart they had grown.

Almost imperceptibly she grew to have what her mother called a weight problem and her father, baby fat. He offered her Dexamyl for pep, as he put it, since both he and Uncle Larry took a capsule or two every day like vitamins. Jane put on and took off weight like gloves and began not to know what she looked like. She looked at Miss Anderson, her English teacher, who didn't wear a bra, even though she must have been over thirty. To her bleached blond hair and knowing, long-legged swagger Jane turned with fascination; here, she thought, was someone different. Miss Anderson's brother was the biology teacher and he had a plate in his head from the war. It was also rumored that brother and sister were too close. In the classroom the sun shining through the windows reminded Jane of a life that existed elsewhere. Miss Anderson stood at the front of the class, framed by the blackboard, her blond hair and black roots, her white skin, a kind of flag of independence. Her lipstick was a deep red, like her sweater, her mouth moving slowly as she spoke with a drawl that matched her walk. If only, Jane thought, Uncle Larry had met Miss Anderson instead of his new, skinny wife.

For Easter vacation, in her senior year, Larry took her to Florida with his new wife, an ex-dance instructor her mother thought was a tramp, and his daughter from his first marriage. Even in a bathing suit Larry's wife had no hips at all and what stuck out most was the cigarette that hung from her broad mouth. Her lips were big, a feature so unlike the rest of her that Jane considered them almost a deformity. Larry was broad everywhere, and the couple had a Laurel and Hardy quality that made Jane laugh secretly. Her uncle had known Bugsy Siegel—"he'd kill ya if you called him that, though" — and Frank Costello, from a steam room he frequented in the forties and fifties. "Frank saw me at the tables of one of his joints down here and he said to me, 'Larry, what are you doing here? You know these tables are fixed.'" Her uncle told her stories about gangsters and her grandparents that her father never would have. "Your grandmother sent your grandfather away. He was a nice man, too, but we hated him because she told us he was bad." They were on a boat getting terrible sunburns. "Your father took care of me, protected me. He should see a doctor, too, but he won't." Later that day Larry asked her, "How's your sex life?" No one had ever suggested that she might have one. She said she didn't have one. He said he started late too. Larry was driving a rented convertible along the highway that fronted the ocean. The sun was still brilliant.

Jane's sunburn was turning into a third-degree burn right on the spot between her breasts, as if the sun had drilled a hole in her. The sky was a cloudless blue. Larry was in profile against the horizon, and he was speaking to her about things no one else ever had. Jane startled at the mention of her sex life and his, the possibility that they were connected. She felt adult and tragic. That night they went into Miami Beach and Jane fell in love with a college friend of her cousin's. But you only saw him for a minute, her cousin insisted. The next five days, until they went home, Jane ate as if there were no tomorrow.

"Doll," Larry laughed, "slow down. You don't want to look like me, do you?" Jane flew home eight pounds heavier. It was a bad flight, the plane hit an air pocket and dropped a thousand feet. Her uncle stuck some nitroglycerin under her nose. She tried to ignore all the people who'd been drinking heavily before the plane dropped as they vomited around her. This is the way the Romans did it, Jane thought—on purpose. Of course the Romans weren't in a plane flying back from Florida to the suburbs. They did go to the sea, and they ate apples for headaches. And as she thought all this they came closer and closer to earth.

She decided to lose weight, not for her prom, which she wouldn't go to on principle, but for life after it, and found a diet doctor who supplied her with multicolored tablets in small plastic boxes. Jane lost weight and talked constantly or not at all. Asked to be the bridesmaid at her middle sister's wedding, having spent three hours combing her hair, trying to get it right, she didn't smile as she walked down the aisle. Jane's inappropriately sober attitude indicated to her father that his youngest daughter was still unmanageable, and somehow improper. Jane's always been wild, he said. She did lose twenty or so pounds and was as slim as a branch whose leaves had just fallen off.

Her newly married sister fixed her up with a guy who had just graduated from college. He asked her out again and then again. He liked to go into the city and see a play or talk about movies or the war in Vietnam. But when he placed his hand on her breast, Jane felt sick to her stomach. She said she had a headache, as if she had memorized a Victorian manual written for skittish brides. He took her home and kept calling. She dreaded his calls and began to hate him, even though there was nothing hateful about him.

He took her to see *The Balcony* and she spent the whole of the second act in the bathroom, like a Roman. Finally she was mean to him and he never called again. She felt a moment of guilt, then a curious blankness, and then relief.

It was to be Jane's last summer in the suburbs. On graduation night her name was called to accept a $100 award for a mixture of virtues, including good citizenship, given regardless of race or religion. It was the only award so designated and Jane walked forward wondering what, if anything, she had done to deserve it or if she appeared so bland, so colorless that this award had been designed for somebody just like her. Miss Anderson handed her the piece of paper and said, They won't love you if you're good, only if you're rich, and winked.

Jane spent the summer driving around, playing tennis, going to the beach, and fighting with her parents about finding a job. She said there were none. Her mother would say do you mean that in all of Manhattan and Long Island there are no jobs? Her father didn't push her to look for a job the way her mother did. Jane was still taking a lot of pills, to maintain, as the diet doctor recommended. She was the thinnest person in his waiting room. She soaked up the sun as if it were food. Her tennis partners were two sixteen-year-old boys and she played both of them at the same time. She had never gotten so dark and it seemed like an achievement. Jane saw no one from school, but visited Jimmy in the city once or twice. She gave him some of her pills and they drove around Manhattan. She drove him home and she kept driving when no one was on the streets except the police. She drove aimlessly, thinking that the police must be suspicious of her. Expecting to be stopped, she drove slowly. Jane began imagining that her father wanted to kill her and she couldn't sleep.

The days passed. The nights passed. Time disappeared as she stared at her reflection in window and in mirrors. She lay in the sun for hours with nothing on her mind, nothing that she could account for later. Or occasionally an image came to mind. She wrote in her diary: She was walking downstairs and I was at the bottom of the stairs and her hair was long and full. She looked old to me because her breasts were so big and she had a small waist. Maybe that was by comparison. I guess I was about seven and she was sixteen, she was just a little younger than I am now. Jane stopped writing and walked into the bathroom, visualizing the scene, looking at the metal tooth-brush holder which used to be her mirror when she couldn't see over the sink.

The diet doctor stopped her pills suddenly. It was crazy, but it was only later that she knew that, after her father had kicked her out, into the city, where she wanted to live anyway. You'll see, she intoned to Lois as she threw her stuff together, "that these dead shall not have died in vain," the Gettysburg Address coming to mind, her father having recited it so often from the hardcover book he loved. Everything fit into two cardboard boxes; Jane didn't take her yearbook with her name in gold letters on its white cover. She didn't take her tennis racket.

Chapter 2

Grace thought her dolls came alive at night, after midnight, and talked with each other only when she'd fallen asleep. Most likely she'd been told the story of *The Nutcracker Suite*, but Grace, like most children, took stories to heart. She waited up nights, a captive to the secret lives of her dolls, and feared they might say terrible things about her. Against her young will Grace would fall asleep, though sometimes she'd make it past midnight, or what she thought was midnight. To stay awake she danced on her bed, wondering if they were watching. The dolls never spoke, at least she never heard them, and Grace reasoned that they knew she was awake and could wait longer. In a way she never gave up the notion that her dolls came alive. Later, when she stopped playing with them, she forgot it.

Play was Grace's job, the way doing the housework was her mother Ruth's. Ruth did her work defensively, keeping Grace out of the kitchen, telling her humorously to go play as if she were saying go away. Grace found play a lonely job, and she hated her dolls, especially Kitty, the grown-up-looking blond, with breasts much bigger, proportionately, than Grace's, an anomaly not missed by Grace, who found it impossible to mother her. She would hit her dolls for no reason at all, then try to make it up to them. Grace liked animals much better, and any animal, even a stuffed one, was preferable to a doll.

Ruth liked animals better than people. They're loyal, she told Grace, but you can expect more from your family because you're related by blood. Even so, Ruth distrusted her relations. And being related by blood doesn't mean much to a child, but because she was related to them, they were there, rather than other people, at a bungalow colony in her sixth summer. Running out of the cottage naked, Grace liked to wake her relatives early, knocking on their doors and calling out that it was time to get up. They thought of her as uninhibited. With abandon Grace ran into the ocean, carrying an inner tube, and floated as far away from her blood as she could, until her mother called her out of the water and angrily slapped her across the face. You could've drowned made no sense to her; it had no relation to her. Six years later she became afraid of the waves when an especially big one knocked her down and dragged her under. She couldn't catch her breath and she wondered how she had ever not been afraid.

Relatives told Ruth what a bright little girl she had, how cute she was. Ruth accepted their praise with reservations, keeping to herself the thought that these people were after all only family. Grace's true test would come in the world. Fascinated by an older cousin who had, as Ruth put it already developed, as if Grace were a photograph still in the camera, Grace resented having to play with a younger cousin only because they were the same age. Ruth told her husband, Grace doesn't know how to play.

The sand, the ocean, the bugs, the snakes. The people with newly red flesh advertising their bodies in bathing suits that exposed the red and the white, the lines demarcating the private parts. Grace even thought of herself as an explorer, a Columbus coming upon a new world. She took long walks with her older brother, Richard, who had been mandated by Ruth to look after her. Each time they set off they went farther and farther, miles and miles away. Grace thought, not exactly clear what a mile was, but farther than she had ever been from her mother. A sense of danger accompanied her like a best friend. Once upon a time there appeared a stream, so wide that it had a bridge across it, and standing on it was a boy Richard's age. He was holding a burlap sack that had kittens in it, he told them, and then he hurled the bag over the bridge. Grace and Richard stood by, dumb, and watched the bag disappear under the water, bit by bit. Finally it was all gone. Richard told her that farmers were like that, that they had a different attitude toward animals, because they raised them to eat or to kill. "Then I'll never be a farmer," she said belligerently, "if they kill kittens." Richard laughed at the idea. Grace announced that she would never live in the country, "if that's the way people are." And she never did, though her reasons were different when she got older. She said the country made her nervous. In her memory the boy who drowned the kittens became like a picture in a family photo album, still and frozen. But the scene was too horrible to have been real, and Grace often thought it was a dream.

Grace missed her room at home. Small as it was, it was hers and she grew to love it as if it were human. After school she'd kiss its floor, with passion, pursing her lips, opening her mouth slightly, the way movie stars did. In this room she invoked her fantasies, directing herself to choose the best one, going over it and over it, it always giving her pleasure. She directed her friend Celia too. They had a special game and Grace was tyrannical about being the girl, letting Celia be her only once in a while. Celia the man would come upon Grace the girl, unaware, innocent and grab her from behind. The girl would pretend to fight and then abandon herself to the man. They enacted this scene over and over again, Celia fighting Grace more and more about getting the chance to be the girl. They lived in the same apartment building, with older brothers the same age, and mothers who didn't like each other. Ruth thought Celia's mother had too many airs. "Like mother, like daughter," Grace's mother intoned.

For one of Ruth's birthdays Grace bought her a cheap pin, a cluster of fake seed pearls around a blue enamel center, which she'd found, all by herself, at a street fair several blocks from home. Returning, she had to pass the gypsies on the corner. They had appeared on the block suddenly, different and strange, and when they beckoned to Grace, waving their arms covered in shiny red and blue material, she hesitated, stuck to her spot on the sidewalk. They waved and smiled, their white teeth bright against their dark skin. Grace stared and ran, not knowing why they wanted her, or what they would do with her. Ruth was given her present. She said it was ugly and that she'd never wear it. She opened the top drawer of her mahogany dresser, put the pin with other junk jewelry and shut the drawer with finality. As she shut it she told Grace that it was important to tell the truth. The gypsies wore much uglier jewelry. Weeks later Grace dreamt that her mother was killed by a runaway train. Ruth had been tied to the tracks and no one could save her. That made sense because Ruth always refused help. If you do things by yourself, you won't owe anyone anything, she'd tell Grace. Grace woke screaming and asked to sleep with her mother, who told her she was being silly. And added, You're not a baby anymore.

There was something calm about Celia, as if she had a big secret that she wouldn't tell anyone, most of all Grace. Grace always wanted to find out what she knew. When Celia refused to play their special game anymore, saying they were too old—they were now ten —they set up a make-believe office, reviving Celia's father's dead business files and ledgers. Their business was an imaginary army of women. The names of their female soldiers were alphabetized and placed on cards in a small metal box. From Celia's room they sent their soldiers on maneuvers and they punished and rewarded them as they had done their dolls. But added to their older responsibilities—discipline and feeding—was administration, and they took to it as if called to it. Grace was stricter, more punitive than Celia, who wanted to give the girls longer leaves and more dances. Grace no longer danced on her bed when listening to the radio, and, wearing real baby clothes that Ruth bought because they were more economical than doll's clothes, Tiny Tears and Kitty sat on a shelf in the farthest part of Grace's closet, as if that shelf were her childhood.

Childhood ends in all different ways. One way was by understanding her parent's fights, which she watched like a spectator at a tennis game. "If you don't like the way we live," her father yelled, "get a job." "I've had your children and you're going to support me," her mother yelled. He slapped her and she slapped him. Or it ends when the facts of life, as they were called, are flaunted in your mirror, at a stage called puberty, a dumb word Grace thought. Or childhood ends on the playground, where she once played potsy and now was being shown pornography, a word she knew without knowing how but didn't tell Little Louie. He shuffled the pastel-pink playing cards much too fast, so that the naked bodies blurred as if they too were shocked. Little Louie had dark circles under his eyes Grace attributed, as she did his diminutive size, to early coffee drinking. He was a naughty, ugly boy, in love with Grace, who didn't know it. They got reported to the principal —Grace's first brush with the law—and he threatened to call in their parents. Louie acted as if he didn't care, but Grace cried and begged the principal not to. The principal let the kids off as though he were commuting a death sentence to life. Grace could never again face the principal, and Louie could never again face Grace, and she will have no memory of his presence on that playground or in her life ever again after that time. She was convinced now that she was a sinner, because she had looked at dirty pictures. When she had asked her mother, Do you, we, believe in sin? Ruth had said yes, because there is evil in the world. Real evil, Grace asked, like the devil? Ruth looked at her daughter seriously. She didn't believe in talking down to children. There may not, she said, be an actual devil, but there is a lot of evil in the world, a lot of sin, and sometimes I wonder. It's best not to trust people too much. Grace couldn't trust Louie; he was a little devil, getting her into trouble, making her sin. Grace didn't tell anyone what she'd seen, learning to distinguish between good and bad knowledge.

Now she too had a secret, a secret she took to camp with her, where she was sent away for three weeks. An unwilling camper— Ruth told her it was time to grow up—Grace lived in a bunk with seven other girls her age, but her friend was Sandy, an older girl of fifteen who had a broken nose and biceps. All the girls thought Sandy was strange, but she was devoted to Grace, doing favors for her, taking pictures of her in front of the bunk. And late at night, giving her back rubs, and Grace knew her power, another secret. She played the special game when things were innocent, because one was unaware, or thought to be unaware. Sandy went home unacknowledged. Years later Grace wondered what had happened to all those pictures of her looking so cute, and what had happened to Sandy.

That summer her breasts grew and Grace mailed away for "Sally, Mary and Kate Wondered," a twelve-page pamphlet with diagrams and line drawings of the girls in the title. When it finally happened, Ruth announced it at dinner. Richard looked like he was about to laugh and her father cleared his throat and said, Now you're a woman. Grace stared at him, then continued making drawings on a paper napkin, remembering that two years before she thought she might be an adult. Out shoe-shopping, the salesman had measured her feet and told her mother Grace was now a size five. "We're going," Ruth stated, as if insulted by the salesman, who had always measured Grace's feet. She pulled Grace after her, leaving him with a shoe in his hand. "That's an adult size," Ruth whispered to Grace, marching her toward that other world, Ruth's favorite shoe store, and Grace felt her childhood had reached another ridiculous end. Now, at the table two years later, her father pronounced her a woman. Was there such a difference, she wondered as she colored in, with a Crayola, the tiny patterns on the paper napkin. Richard was horrible, she thought, looking at his familiar face, but one of his friends was so cute, Grace died whenever he came to the apartment. She hoped he wouldn't say anything to him about her being a woman.

All the girls stopped speaking to Grace. It was her turn. The last year before high school, the girls ignored her for months and months, way beyond the normal time for exclusion. It did something to Grace, walking to school alone, being ignored in the halls, or whispered about behind her back. "You must have done something wrong," Ruth said, perceiving her daughter's imperfections as personal insults. Even her brother assumed it was her fault, but he took her to a movie now and then, meting out the angry sympathy a seventeen-year-old boy offers a younger sister. She made friends with a nice, unpopular girl called Marlene, who was striking in her indifference to her unpopularity. This distinguished her in Grace's eyes, and while Grace couldn't understand how she could stand it, she admired her for it. The boys kept talking to her and asking her to parties she couldn't attend because the girls would be there. Grace was set strangely upon her own devices.

During the trouble, as her family called it, as if Grace were pregnant out of wedlock rather than out of sympathy with her friends, she tried to see herself as enduring a trial by fire from which she had to emerge stronger. She read more than she ever had and wrote down sentences that applied to victims like herself, to read over and over when the phone rang and she knew if she picked it up someone would just hang up. Her dog Lady kept her company. Ruth had gotten Grace the dog three years before, for her birthday, mother and daughter still linked by their love of animals, although Ruth got rid of them when they got in the way or were too much trouble.

Lady was pregnant when they rescued her from the ASPCA, and Ruth said that's why she was abandoned. Terrible people do things like that to defenseless animal, but they'll be punished. Every time Grace hurt herself Ruth said that God was punishing her. When she was older she asked Ruth if she believed in God. Ruth told her she was an agnostic, someone who doesn't know, was the way she put it. She was washing dishes. Then why do you say that God is punishing me, if you're not sure? Ruth put out her cigarette, which was wet with a rosy stain where she sucked it. If I don't believe in God it doesn't mean that you shouldn't or don't have to. Ruth looked out the window over the sink. I'm an agnostic because an agnostic is a realist. You will be too. Grace considered this a compliment, since they fought most of the time, even during the trouble. She repeated the comment to Celia, who had continued to speak to her, but not at school, where the trouble might at any time happen to her. The two friends didn't discuss the terms of Celia's neutrality; it just existed.

Just as suddenly as the trouble had begun it stopped, and Grace was allowed back into the fold. But this was never, never going to happen to her again. Never. For she had determined that when it was over—the word over had magical properties—when it was over, she would have emerged a new person, a girl much too irresistible and tough for that to happen to ever again.

The house was never quiet. Ruth and Grace fought about everything. Grace took her dinner in front of the TV or in her room. She hated the way her mother chewed, she hated the sound. Ruth called her names and dumped her dresser drawers, and Grace fought back by ignoring her, or giving her dirty looks. You're bad, you and your stupid friends, her mother would yell. Grace had been told by her algebra teacher that when she was good, she was very very good, but when she was bad she was better. Now that Grace was a freshman in high school, or a fresh girl, as Ruth put it, when she got to school, home didn't exist.

She wanted to be the most popular girl in her class. With the boys or with the girls, Celia asked tartly. Both, Grace said. Are you going to let them feel you up? Maybe, Grace answered, if I feel like it.

Seeing herself as leading a double life, not unlike Philbrick in I Led Three Lives, she kept to herself at home, smiling very little, staying in her now too small and messy room. She kept the door shut. It didn't have a lock. Grace could hear her mother outside, moving around, doing things. She talked to her dog, and waited for phone calls, or made some. You talk on the phone too much, Ruth would say angrily. And what happened to that nice girl, Marlene? It's none of your business, Grace would say, looking for food in the refrigerator, finding only raisins. You never buy anything good to eat, she flung at her mother, returning to her room, closing the door hard behind her. Ruth was gaining weight and wearing housedresses most of the time. Grace followed her diet, and although she was thin, she thought she looked fat.

Your room's a mess, Ruth yelled, you can't leave it like that. Leave me alone, Grace yelled back, slamming the front door, going to meet Celia at the diner. As she walked she pulled herself together, into her other self, the popular girl she was when she wasn't at home. Celia surprised Grace because other people simply liked her while Grace continued to feel two ways about her all the time. But she was already there, in the diner, waiting, as she had always been in Grace's life, just there. Grace ordered a bran muffin. Bran muffins were delicate food, the right thing to eat, and not fattening. Celia and she watched who came in and who walked out and drank a lot of coffee, Little Louie's cautionary dark circles and stature absent even from memory. Grace drank carefully and without sound. My mother tried to hit me again but I held her hand, she reported sarcastically to Celia. Grace's face hardened. I hate her guts. Just then a cute boy walked in and Celia didn't have to reply, while Grace's face recomposed itself into a prettier picture. Celia didn't know what to say anyway.

Grace watched Celia's eyes widen and freeze, then set; she enjoyed shocking people, or scaring them. Her drive for popularity was hindered by a bluntness that bordered on meanness. Celia would tell her that some of the girls didn't understand that she was just being honest. Girls are so critical, Grace told Celia, meaningfully. She envied Celia's ease with friends, her girlfriends, and said, I think I like boys better, and watched Celia's eyelids open and close like a venetian blind. Envy made Grace feel weak and sinful, and she didn't like not feeling strong. She prided herself on being reckless.

When Grace got called down to the principal's office to discuss her grades and her attitude, he told her she was sullen and uncooperative. My aptitude is much higher than my performance, she repeated in the coffee shop, to which one of the guys, a senior, responded, Did you ask him about his performance? Her cool face reddened as she drank in their attention with her coffee; later, the senior asked her out. Why not, she answered, as if she were thinking it over, weighing his performance neutrally. "Did you let him kiss you?" Ruth asked. "Sure," Grace answered. "Where?" her mother asked. "Where do you think?" and Grace slammed out of the house. A gunshot of fear traveled up her mother's body from her toes to the top of her head where it settled as wounded anger.

In high school sex was war, a conventional war about the conventions. There were skirmishes at the breast, the line below the pantie, at the thigh, and finally the assault upon the Maginot Line, the vagina. And for these advances there was the creation of an adolescent military strategy that the boys and the girls developed separately, at separate tables, and then enacted with one another, following or not following the codes of war, at parties, in cars, on their absent parents' beds.

Just before Grace was fifteen she met a nineteen-year-old drop-out who worked in a boutique not far from the coffee shop. He had full lips and slanted eyes and told risqué jokes. He did crazy things, like putting a two-way mirror in the dressing room, and Grace fell hard. He told her she was cute and gave her a lavender shirt that he stole from the store, her first present from a boyfriend. The first time he stood her up, she waited up all night in her room, not really believing that he was doing this to her, that the phone hadn't rung, the way it hadn't when she was in the eighth grade, or if it rang, only to torment her. He called a few days later, and made an excuse which she accepted while seeming to have difficulty remembering what the infraction had been, it had been so slight. When she saw him again Grace kissed him with abandon and an open mouth and he pushed her away. You shouldn't kiss like that, he warned, you're supposed to be a nice girl. And he came around less often, and when he did he brought his friends, who acted like guards in a recently neutralized corridor, the battle having ended in a stalemate. Severed slowly over time, the attachment weakened and disappeared. She didn't want to be a nice girl. Grace liked kissing boys with abandon.

I made my bed, Grace called out as she left for school, in answer to Ruth's question. But it was not made and Ruth saw red and dumped her daughter's drawers once more, dumped them in a single movement, and marched out as if there were something blocking her way. She hated being lied to, by Grace, her husband, her son, anyone. She complained to her husband, Grace could make all our beds in the amount of time it takes her to put on eye makeup. Her husband pulled off his pants. He said she was bad, as if Grace's behavior were beyond his ken, as if he were describing someone from a tribe in Asia whose customs made him sick. Is that all you can say? Ruth asked, rubbing out her cigarette with dissatisfaction. Her husband glanced at her. Something might explain the intensity of her discontent, but not seeing it he turned over on his stomach and waited to fall asleep.

On the nights that Grace couldn't sleep, Lady kept her company. When she took a bath Lady hovered by, upset that Grace was wet, and licked her like a puppy. If occurred to Grace that Lady might lick her there, if she directed her dog the way she had once directed her fantasies and Celia. Lady's tongue was pink, not that rough, but she didn't teach her to do it because the idea that she needed a dog was humiliating. She remembered that when reading *A Stone for Danny Fisher* she used to put her finger in her vagina and rub it until small pieces of her vagina—or what she thought was her vagina—rolled into balls and stuck to her fingers. She learned that men who ran candy stores liked to see a young girl's breasts pressed against the glass cabinet and that, if the girl did that she could get some candy, or something for free, or for very little.

Boys learn the value of a dollar by taking girls out on dates, Ruth told her, and girls have to learn the value of a dollar too. Grace was forced to baby-sit for neighborhood families. Usually she took care of older children, but one night she was hired to care for an infant, the son of a young married couple. It was a night job. She turned on the TV and heard the baby crying. She let him cry a while, then went to talk to him, but he didn't stop. She walked out and turned up the volume. The baby kept crying. She tried to change his diapers but he wriggled out of her grip and screamed as if she were killing him. She saw red. Shut up, she yelled, but the baby yelled louder and her grip got tighter. Grace slapped his little ass very hard, leaving a white handprint. He screamed louder and she left the room. She couldn't stand the sound. She ate all the junk food in the refrigerator, and decided that babies, like dolls, were for other girls.

While Grace was determined not to have children, she was equally dead set against remaining a virgin. She had passed through some of the preliminaries described to Celia as no big deal. She didn't really care that her reputation was shot to hell, like her souvenir target from shooting live bullets at Coney Island. She wasn't, after all, going to live in Brooklyn her whole life, about that she was certain. She chose an older guy who had graduated from high school, gone early to Vietnam, and returned to the neighborhood, a man, she thought, he'd have to be. He was necessarily different from the other boys and wouldn't talk about the war, so he, too, had a secret. Her intensity was equal to his, if coming from a place where he had never fought. She was intent upon showing abandon, by ceding herself to the enemy, and very deliberately surrendering, without knowing the terms of the peace. She told Celia that she hadn't bled.

Her last winter in high school was as cold a one as she could recall. But even on the coldest days, visiting the zoo in Central Park was a relief, a small vacation from her crowd and her reputation. It was so cold that the skin on her ankles dried, stretching too tightly across the bone like leather. The skin cracked and bled, something Grace imagined happened only to old people. After a hot chocolate in the cafeteria, Grace walked toward the polar bears lying in the winter sun, their massive coats keeping them warm. As nature intended,

Ruth might've put it thought Grace, as she pulled her coat closer to her. She walked past them, into the park.

Everything in the park seemed sharp, crisp, enclosed by the cold blue sky. The landscape was a jigsaw puzzle whose pieces could all break apart if touched. From nowhere fifty or more stray cats moved toward her in a group. They were skinny and sick. She thought they might devour her, and though it was crazy, she ran back to the cafeteria and bought as many frankfurters as she had money for, returning to the cats who were waiting, it seemed, for her. She tore the meat and bread into little pieces and threw the food to them. Tribute, or bribe, or sacrifice, the pieces were gone in no time. Turning to leave, Grace saw an old woman coming down the path. She said she fed them every day, that the park wanted to get rid of them, kill them. I won't let them, the frail white-haired woman declared. The ASPCA really hates animals, she told Grace. Had Grace been on speaking terms with her mother, she might have told her that.

Celia applied to college, but Grace's grades were low, and it looked like she might not get into one. I may become an artist or an actress, she told Celia. I love movies. And circuitously hearing about Grace and the Vietnam vet, her brother had a talk with her in which he warned that giving it away wasn't going to get her anywhere. "You did it when you were my age," she said. "I'm a guy," he said, "it's different." "Fuck difference," she said.

It was during that same cold winter, in her seventeenth year, that Grace held a kitchen knife in her hand and pointed it at her mother. Undoubtedly this is a scene repeated in many households, or so Grace reasoned, for she decided it wasn't so strange to want to kill one's mother. She never leaves me alone. When Grace lifted the knife—she was at the sink—Ruth stopped yelling. The effect on Ruth was immediate and in a way funny. Grace had never seen her mother so much at a loss. The look satisfied Grace and she set the knife down slowly, her eyes fixed as sternly as she could make them on her mother's startled face. Grace stared hard at Ruth like a gunfighter in a showdown.

It's one thing for her to yell fuck you at me, Ruth told her husband, it's another thing for her to threaten me with a knife. But nothing at all was done to Grace, whose behavior had pushed her in her parents' eyes, into a territory that transformed her from just bad to perhaps crazy. What punishment could fit the crime of attempted matricide? These weren't Greek queens and kings whose realms were at stake. These were middle-class white people with problems. Grace felt that she had made a lasting impression.

Chapter 3

Hilda was Emily's second piano teacher. How Emily knew Hilda was a lesbian, though she was only eight and not living among sophisticates, is something she's not sure about even today. How she learned was more mysterious than what she learned.

Hilda's partner taught piano also and her name sounded like Mr. Mars when said quickly. She wore grey suits, had short white-grey hair, and her face was round and soft, with a benevolent smile. She drove the old Dodge that waited for Hilda after lessons. To Emily the car and the partner were one.

Emily loved the two piano teachers, particularly Hilda. She wore delicate blouses and full skirts, whose fabrics, in many different colors and patterns, were often like fields of flowers around her arms and legs. She didn't seem to try to match things, it was her way of being natural. She was tall with big breasts and given to hugging Emily's father to her impressive chest where his head would land with embarrassment. He'd blush and she'd say how adorable he was.

The whole family liked Hilda, who was strange and remarkably white-skinned. The skin on her hands was so pale that her veins showed blue like rivulets. Her nails were cut short and round, and looked as if they never touched anything even though she played the piano every day. Hilda visited only once a week, but she was important to Emily. For one thing she was different from her family.

Emily's family were FDR Democrats. Hilda appeared at one lesson wearing a rhinestone pin, made of initials, on her flowered blouse. Emily asked, "What is that?" "I-K-E," Hilda announced. "I-K-E"? Emily repeated, not putting it together. "Ike, Ike," Hilda pronounced vigorously. Emily was stunned. Hilda was a Republican. She even wrote songs for Ike. So did her partner with a man's name when said fast. How could she be for Ike? Ike and not Adlai. Disenchanted, Emily withdrew somewhat from her piano teacher. This heresy, not Hilda's affection for women, put a first wall between the girl and the woman. Emily continued to take piano lessons but began to think that Hilda might not know everything.

No one had ever mentioned lesbianism to Emily; it didn't exist as good or bad to her. But Republicans—her family was definitely against the Republicans who, she imagined, must be bad, like the Yankees. Emily had become a Dodger fan when she was three and one of her playmates asked what team she liked. She didn't have a team yet and asked her father, who said he was for the Dodgers.

Emily's best friend Nora also took lessons from Hilda. The best friends met when they were five. It was, in Emily's memory a formal first meeting. They stood cautiously behind their respective mother's dresses and said hello. In what seemed like no time they were best friends living, as they did, just around the corner from each other in houses that were almost the same painted in different colors. It's funny that they met behind their mother's dresses, for it was then a literal truth that they stood in their mothers' shadows. The two women were friends for a while and then Emily's mother stopped speaking to Nora's mother because of something she said. Emily never knew what.

When they were five Nora was not yet homely and Emily did not seem unsure of herself. Though it was Nora who struck people as uncertain and nervous, it was Emily, more often than not who apologized to Nora when they fought. At a young age Emily saw herself as slavish but didn't know how to keep Nora's love.

At six Nora used to hide under the kitchen table, covering her heart with both hands, expecting it to stop at any moment. She feared death early; she was precocious that way. Emily used to stand near the kitchen table, looking down, while Nora huddled under it. She tried to convince her that she wasn't going to die. Nora's parents sent her to a doctor. Her mother waited outside his office. After a while Nora stopped hiding under the table and clutching her heart and her parents said she didn't need to see the doctor anymore.

Emily and Nora learned to laugh together so that it sounded like they were hee-hawing. When they didn't go to camp together, they went to the beach with Nora's mother. Emily's mother said she didn't like the beach. It turned out she was afraid of the ocean. At eight Nora was skinny and awkward; Emily was round and blond, becoming beautiful through no effort of her own. It was a difference between them and Emily ignored it. Nora maintained an unwitting power over Emily, who had many fears.

One of Emily's fears was the forest. It fronted her house and was behind Nora's house, a kind of nobody's land that belonged to the kids. It became the jungle, the bicycle path that dared her to go through it, the hunting ground. Later it was cleared so that a dull family could build a house and live in it. Emily even suffered the indignity of baby-sitting for them. Emily, Nora, and Nora's brothers used the forest as a location for their first 8mm film, which employed as its main actors a cocker spaniel belonging to a neighbor and themselves appearing and disappearing mysteriously in front of the camera. The camera caught one of Nora's and Emily's fights. Years later Emily couldn't remember what the fight was about, but was surprised to see herself fighting back.

Nora's brother, Paul, who was the middle child and also a student of Hilda's, wanted to see their vaginas. So did his friend, who seemed like an old man to Emily. The boys showed the girls their penises. The girls were dressed up, Paul being the producer of the event, and Emily felt it wasn't fair, the boys looking the same while the girls had fabrics thrown over them and lipstick put on their already red lips. Then they opened their legs and the boys looked in. No one had ever looked in Emily before; it made her feel strange. She wondered whether there was something more peculiar about Paul's looking at his sister's vagina, but she didn't know. The fact that it was and had to remain a secret disturbed her more than opening her legs to them. The event disappeared into her memory the way they all appeared and disappeared in the movie.

Hilda preferred Emily to Nora, who rarely practiced and came late to lessons. But Paul was her favorite because he was noticeably tortured. At the age of fourteen he couldn't throw a ball, moved slowly, and was far from lanky. Paul's father had, over the years, taken this son to the ballpark, thrown a few balls to him, and realized it was hopeless, like a dog that can't be trained. This hopelessness communicated itself to Paul, who was a mensch and adored by Hilda. She'd exclaim to Emily, "I adore Paul." Emily watched their relationship and was jealous of its intimacy. She was sure they talked on the piano bench about subjects she couldn't broach with the piano teacher.

When Nora's nose developed an adult bump, accentuating her small eyes, she was at last truly homely. She didn't seem to care and Emily and she didn't discuss looks. The two girls read lots of books and wrote the best compositions in class. Nora's were better than Emily up until the eighth grade, or so Emily thought. They were as close as two girls could be.

Emily was positive, by now, that Hilda talked to Paul about love and sex. She was sure that Hilda revealed herself to Paul in a way she never had with Emily. Then suddenly, Paul and Hilda weren't close anymore. Something had happened and Emily didn't know what. Paul still took his lessons, like medicine, but there was no more conspiring. Emily figured that one of them must have said or discovered something really bad about the other, the way her mother must've about Nora's mother. Something awful happens and people stop liking each other. Emily worried that Nora would turn from her for no reason, or for reasons she couldn't fathom and no one talked about. Her mother said, "There's nothing to fear but fear itself."

Nora and Emily read as much as they could because they wanted to be writers when they grew up. Girls with promise, their teachers said. Nora read adventure stories and books about early American patriots like Nathan Hale. Emily took out every biography of a woman that she could find in the school library. There weren't that many and the women were all of a kind, good women who had served well. Emily liked Abigail Adams best because she was something of a troublemaker. Like Nora's mother, who had gone back to college to become a lawyer. Emily spent a lot of time in Nora's house, sometimes eating her breakfast there before school. She told her mother there were better cereals at Nora's. Nora rarely finished what was on her plate or in her bowl and her mother would say, "That's why your blouses fall out of your skirts." Hilda didn't approve of the way Nora came to her lessons—she was sloppy—but Nora didn't care what Hilda thought. She was obstinate in a sullen way and quit her lessons when Hilda became too demanding.

Emily wondered what Nora's mother thought of her; Nora didn't like her mother or Emily's mother. They were in the eighth grade now, and in separate classes for the first time. They still took the same yellow school bus driven by fat Freddie, who always waited for Nora, who was habitually late. Nora and Emily vowed that being in different classes wouldn't change anything.

Hilda chose Emily to accompany her at the annual piano recital. She had to learn "I Could Have Danced All Night." Emily knew she was supposed to feel honored at having been chosen but she felt embarrassed. She hated the song and having to appear in public.

Hilda tried to reassure her, but Emily was miserable. She didn't appreciate Hilda as much as she once had, especially since Nora had quit. She had been taking her lessons seriously for five years. One Tuesday she announced to Hilda, in the angular and uncompromising way that youthful decisions are both made and delivered, that she wanted to stop. Emily made some excuses about being a freshman and having homework and both knew she was lying. Hilda argued with restraint but didn't wring her hands. There's not much a piano teacher can do. After the last lesson her partner picked her up, as she always did, in the old Dodge, and off they went out of Emily's young life. It didn't occur to Emily that she might not see Hilda again.

Nora's brothers were both away at college and Nora was glad. Her new high school friends had less money than her family, but they dressed tough and smoked grass and danced better than anyone she knew. Emily and she still talked on the phone but they didn't see each other as much. Nora fell in love with a black guy called Eddie who was strong and handsome and older, and who didn't seem to notice that she wasn't beautiful. She wore her skirts shorter than the other fourteen-year-old white girls and walked as if she were dancing. When Nora phoned Emily to tell her of her love for Eddie, black and from the wrong part of town, Emily was surprised that Nora had to tell her, shocked that she didn't know it before the way she knew everything about Nora. Nora was a part of her life, like an arm or a leg. Maybe they weren't best friends anymore. Emily feared for Nora's life in high school, where even walking through the halls to the next class caused Emily humiliation. One time she asked an older boy if he had the time and he said if you've got the place. But she admired Nora's visible passion.

When Nora broke up with Eddie he broke into her house, the house he had never been allowed to visit. Nora called Emily and told her, saying now her parents knew everything. They sent her to another psychiatrist. Emily had heard about approved psychiatrists who told parents everything, the way one had done to her friend Beth. Beth had been made love to by a boy who called her Baby and wrote her letters from military academy. Then the letters stopped. Beth gained and lost weight, started sleeping with many boys, and covered her round and pink baby face with rouge and makeup. Beth's shrink told her parents that she wasn't a virgin and they watched her like hawks. Emily thought that Beth would never recover and it was a caution to her. She read about love and listened—Emily was a good listener—and gave her friends advice that she gleaned from books and a cautious spirit.

Nora had a nose job when she was sixteen, the bump she had seemed not to care about was gone. She told Emily, when they met, that she wasn't going to be a writer. They were standing on the corner in front of the house that had replaced the forest. Peter walked by them. Back then he had been Emily's boyfriend, a slight dark boy with big, meaningful eyes. His features, as he grew older and bigger, enlarged, leaving traces of someone once vulnerable, but Emily had to squint her eyes to see him like that. His older sister was rumored to be wild, but when they were children she used to dress Nora and Emily in costumes of her own design. They'd do that on rainy afternoons, while Peter sat in a corner; everyone said his older sister was the creative one. Emily spent part of fourth and fifth grades playing kissing games in Peter's closet. They also passed afternoons climbing into houses that were under construction along with Harvey, an overweight boy with a reading problem. Harvey fell through an unfinished attic floor, and they ran away. The contractor gathered together all the kids on the block and demanded to know who'd done it. There was an uncomfortable silence until Peter stepped forward and said his mother had taught him never to lie and that Harvey had done it. That ended climbing in houses and Emily was forced to look at Peter with new eyes and juggle, like an acrobat, the contradictory values of truth and friendship. Their kissing games halted when Peter's mother made slighting remarks about Emily's character to her mother, overheard by Emily, who experienced deep humiliation. Peter walked past Emily and Nora as if this history had never existed between them. He waved his hand brusquely, as befitted an upperclassman. Emily waved back and turned from the sight of him, and the memory, to Nora, who looked so different with her new nose.

Her mother had taken a part-time job and wasn't at home when Emily got there and walked past the piano that no longer was played. We should sell it, her mother would say. I may play it again, was the answer. Emily mother was working in the local community house, the only interracial center in town. Emily turned on the television and opened her book. One eye watched the movie, the other, her paperback on the American Revolution. Revolution or evolution, her young male history teacher had asked. The question plagued Emily, who could find no easy answer for it, yes or no, and it seemed to be both. But was that an answer? The movie was *Duel in the Sun* and Emily was distracted from the American Revolution. Gregory Peck, who she thought looked a little like her father, and Jennifer Jones, madly in love, dying, crawling toward each other for one last embrace, after they'd shot each other. They loved each other but they had to destroy each other. That was as big a problem as the American Revolution and exciting, in a different way, from thinking, for instance, that it's impossible to know anything for sure.

Emily's mother complained about having to work, but she had a lot more to talk about since she started the job. And Emily had the house to herself for several hours every day, which made her feel almost grown-up. Her mother now knew all the black leaders of the community and gave a few parties that were really integrated. She's probably the talk of the town, Emily thought. Her mother seemed oblivious and it made Emily proud. Her mother never mentioned civil rights. It was as if she was doing what she was doing just because she was who she was and no one was going to tell her who to be friends with. Indeed her mother sometimes seemed oblivious to anyone's rights but her own. Still, Emily thought that on the face of it it made her mother more like a person than a mother.

She had figured out that the American Revolution was best called a rotation. It combined both aspects that she so desperately wanted to mesh. She wrote ten handwritten pages and gave them to her teacher, becoming her history teacher's favorite student, not because she did everything right, but because she argued ferociously about issues most kids understood as academic. "It's life or death to her," the teacher told his wife. "Very peculiar girl. Maybe she's in love with me." "Maybe," his wife said. "It could be a schoolgirl crush, or it could be something else."

Her parents thought she stayed in too much, and Nora's thought she went out too much, but since the ex-best friends' mothers still weren't talking to each other, and Emily still didn't know why, they didn't compare notes, but complained in the privacy of their bedrooms that the other teenager was better adjusted.

Nora's remodeled nose gave her the feeling that now she was like everybody else, and so she went to more and more parties, where she met more and more boys. Emily went to a few parties, to keep up appearances, but preferred to read about them in books. She's not normal, her father would say. Oh, she's probably normal enough, her mother would say, but not to Emily. To Emily her parents presented a united front. Why can't you be more normal? The one thing Emily wanted less and less was to be more normal.

Emily found herself thinking about Hilda. The piano had been sold, over her protests, and she mourned its passing as if it had been alive.

Hilda had been different. Now the living room had a big hole in it. It has no heart anymore, Emily felt, no heart. She started to dream about Hilda and wished off and on to find her, as if by finding her she could always be a child. But she didn't even open the telephone book to call her. It was more like a novel that was living in her head and at the end of it there Hilda would be and everything would be all right again.

They were now seniors and both girls were supposed to apply to college. Nora got into a not very good one that she'd drop out of, she told herself, as soon as she met someone. Emily, as much as she said she wanted go to college, applied late everywhere, and ended up at a city university. She'd have to live at home in the city. She discovered that she didn't care; she didn't want to go away to school. She told her friends that she'd much rather go to a school that didn't look like a school. "She's too much of a homebody," her father complained. "It's not normal." "She'll be all right," her mother said. "Once she's in college. She won't be so out of place there."

In Nora's first year she met someone who was a senior and going to be an accountant. Emily was introduced to him during intercession. In the room where she had once hidden under the table saying her heart was going to stop, Nora announced: "I love him and I'm dropping out. We're getting married." Emily regarded the object of Nora's quest as a curiosity. This is what she'd been waiting for. He seemed nice enough, but looked like he'd aged very quickly for his years. She wondered what Nora's mother, who had finally gotten her law degree, thought of him. For some reason or other, Emily didn't go to the wedding.

Emily wasn't sure why she wasn't living at home anymore with her parents. At the same time, she was convinced that in her day and age it would be completely wrong not to leave home. She moved out almost automatically to live in another woman's apartment.

She was lying in bed and didn't want to get up and leave her room. She was remembering things. She lived in a small room that had once been for the maid. The woman who rented her the room was a widow whose husband had died eight years before Emily moved in. But, for a while, Emily thought he had just died because the widow, Edith, talked about him every day as if he'd just slipped away. Edith had two grown daughters who hardly ever wanted to spend any time with her. It was odd to see the other side of it. Considering how much they didn't want to see her, Edith did all right. She thought about her husband, saw friends, went to work, concerts, and plays, and watched television. She didn't want to remarry. Emily's mother would tell her that people who didn't remarry showed that they didn't like being married the first time, otherwise, she'd sum up, They'd do it again, wouldn't they? Emily gave Edith the benefit of the doubt. Maybe no one could fill the dead man's shoes, if he were so wonderful, the way she said, for more than a night or two.

Emily ventured into herself with time on her hands. She plucked her eyebrows and wore a red flannel nightgown. The telephone was under her skinny bed. She was missing her classes. She had a pile of books on her bed and turned from one to the other, fixing on the life of Dante Gabriel Rossetti with pictures. Then went back to her eyebrows, wanting to remove them all. When they met in the kitchen Edith asked Emily what she'd done to her eyebrows and what was she doing in bed all day? Edith kept busy. The phone under the bed rang and Emily was allowed to disappear, back into her room, back to bed. I think I've started the back-to-bed movement and I may never get up, she said to Christine, her best friend. Christine tweezed her hairline to make her brow higher. There were short black stubbles along the edge of her scalp that she pulled out as fast as she could get hold of them with tweezers. Emily was short, Christine tall, and when they went for walks they'd point out other best friends who looked roughly the way they did. They'd see themselves in all kinds of people. Christine found it hard to get Emily out of her room.

Edith's large prewar apartment was kept dark, long halls past unused bedrooms always unlit. One time Emily walked right into Edith's door, at the end of the hall, and knocked on it by accident with her head. She liked to watch TV with Edith. Edith would talk during the old movies and tell stories about her dead husband. "He could cry at movies," she'd say, "he was a very unusual man."

Lying on the oversized marriage bed that Edith would never sell, Emily listened to her heart's content. They shared Royal Lunch crackers and beer, until Edith announced she had to get up early and Emily left the room, walking again in the dark to her own.

Emily read Rossetti for sentimental instruction; people felt differently from her. When she was reading *Oblomov* he appeared by the side of her bed. She had awakened in the middle of a dream and there he sat wearing a brown velvet smoking jacket. His legs were crossed and he stared at her, pointedly. She opened and closed her eyes. He didn't disappear. She turned on the light and he was gone. Maybe I do stay in bed too much, she thought, and quit reading the novel.

When she fell back to sleep she dreamt she saw the ocean but all the water had disappeared. She was able to walk on the ocean floor to the other side of the world. She was able to see the underworld. At the other side of the world were groups of girls whose eyes were colorless, or were they blind? The phone rang. Christine insisted that she go to school and that after that they go out. She said Emily had to. Emily said yes and closed her eyes.

Christine picked her up on her motorcycle. When Emily put on the helmet she felt as if she were part of a comedy team. Emily had on her oversized men's army pants that she'd been wearing every day for months, no underpants, a T-shirt, and black heels with silver filigree buckles. She always attended to her shoes. Christine repeatedly told her it didn't matter what she wore because she had such a great face, but Emily wasn't sure. Christine wasn't a bad driver except when she was feeling suicidal, which she always announced to Emily just before they started off. Why do you tell me now, Emily wanted to say. Some of Emily's fears advanced with age, and others receded, like Christine's artificial hairline. She still didn't like high speeds and going over hills, fearing that there wasn't anything on the other side. As a child the very idea of an island frightened her. Because it just stopped, just like that, and the ocean could wash over it. Later that night she and Christine went to a bar; Christine found someone and took him home; Emily took herself home.

For her part Edith watched with neutrality the comings and goings of her young tenant. Since Emily wasn't her daughter, Edith could be relaxed, and sometimes even sided with her against her parents. All Edith demanded was that Emily keep the kitchen clean, not use too many paper towels (Edith dried them to use each twice), turn off the lights, not use her telephone, and for the rest, it was her life, she said to herself. Her two children, particularly the younger daughter, who was the baby of the family but not the favorite, were contemptuous and slightly resentful of Edith's friendship with Emily.

Edith acted more or less like a regular person with someone of their generation. Emily recognized the awkwardness of her position, but pretended she didn't. Edith bolstered her self-esteem by inviting Emily to parties where her children could see how well the two of them got along.

Christine had a new boyfriend who occupied her nights, but during her days she faithfully phoned Emily. She wanted Emily to meet him although she said, It's not serious, as if it were a childhood disease. They set aside a Sunday afternoon, but Christine and the guy didn't arrive on time. Then Christine called an hour later and said they'd be there in another hour, and then they didn't show up again. It went like that all afternoon and into the night and Emily was able to lose herself in a book or do her reading for school. She thought about Nora.

On one of her nights out she met a writer named Richard who lived out of town and had a sensitive nature. They didn't see each other often, which suited Emily, but they did write letters, which also suited Emily. He wrote about deprivation, movies, his novel, and boycotting, and she responded in kind. To one of her letters he sent a one-liner: "Touché, I really don't understand, which is precisely why I presume I would say imagine such a lot." In his next he talked about Carol and the man she had married, presumably rather than him, and the different meanings of his "motto of the month, *noli me tangere*." Her answer was an impassioned letter meant to save what was moving palpably away from her. His next ended, "I had a strange feeling while reading your letter, one to which I am not used. It occurred to me that in terms of correspondence you are giving much better than you are getting..." She denied this in hers.

Then his letters stopped. Just a dull, stupid silence, during which Edith and she watched more TV movies and ate more crackers, Edith having waited for her companion's return.

Emily threw herself into her books and was pleased to find comfort in a line from Tonio Kröger, "Only a beginner believes that those who create feel."

Part II

Chapter 4

When Grace contemplated suicide she was about as serious as when she'd threatened to kill her mother. She toyed with the idea, much as she'd played ambivalently with her dolls, or had thought about losing her virginity, an act committed enough times so that she no longer kept count. Losing your virginity is not the same thing as losing your life, her friend Mark chided, even if the sex isn't very good. Grace and Mark held their conversations in dark bars in Providence, Rhode Island, where Grace had moved to be near the art school, which she didn't attend, but which Mark had graduated from, staying in Providence only because, he said, nowhere else in America do the gay bars meet this standard of excellence. Mark was just dying to become a transvestite and had already dyed his hair red, which made him look more like Howdy Doody than Rita Hayworth, Grace told him. Grace was waitressing for money, an occupation, Mark felt, meant only for the fallen. "You haven't fallen far enough," he told her, "you're too young. You'd be heroic if you were older and more tired and working behind a Woolworth counter or in a cafeteria."

Grace eyed him warily. "Maybe I'll be an aide in a mental hospital," she told him. "I'm good around crazy people." His attention turned to the piano player, an overweight man who played like a bored salesman. They were drinking scotch and it was 2 A.M. Sing

"Melancholy Baby," someone yelled, and when the piano player started, Mark began singing too, but just a little behind the piano player, and loudly, to annoy him. Mark claimed he was testing mental health and laughed so hard he lunged forward onto the floor.

But it was Mark who called Grace a fallen angel. Falling reminded her of fucking. Sometimes she'd get an image in her mind of a pair of lips. The lips are full, they purse and reach out, becoming a pair of hands that grab her. She falls, falls into the arms that are lips. A fallen angel, Grace dressed the part. Everything was too tight. She liked to smell her pants after she'd worn them all night, or after she'd fucked. Grace drank some coffee and continued teasing her hair. She drew black lines under those eyes with her thumbs. A guy had told her that late at night under the bar lights her skin was the color of watered-down scotch. Rouge. Mascara. Lipstick. She left her room and walked to work.

Providence could be so creepy. When Mark told her Poe had lived here, she thought it made sense. Grace loved horror, and had always enjoyed scaring people. So and so is frightened of me, a sentence itself employed to shock. There had been a little kid in the next apartment who was very scared...Laughing to herself, women walking past her, Grace watched their breasts. Some breasts moved slowly, almost independent from their bodies, others jumped up and down in time with the legs, the smooth legs covered in nylon. Some breasts moved like waves. Newport wasn't far, Grace was thinking, maybe she'd drive there later that night to go to the beach and look at the waves, whose movement, even in winter, wasn't affected by other things. The cold air was not as strong as the ocean, moving independently of everything. Everyone.

The job at the mental hospital didn't pay much, but Grace took it, feeling that by comparison she'd know she was better off. Institutions are institutions, she told Mark. One of Grace's patients was a twenty-five-year-old woman who was mentally retarded and going blind. Many years ago her parents had given her away—the way people give away dogs, Grace told Mark—and she'd gone from one home to another and had finally landed here, in this place, being visited by an eighteen-year-old girl with not much patience. Madness attracted Grace but this woman repeated the same stories day after day, as did most of the other patients. A glorified and depraved baby-sitter, Mark added that to fallen angel, and Grace's idea of herself was a kind of box of odds and ends, signifying nothing. The nothingness overwhelmed her, thoughts of death slipping into her mind like poison-pen letters. She was always trying to find someone to do something with her. But desire was her best friend, taking her downtown, to bars and clubs, where she'd spend most of her nights.

Suicide is for people who can't stand not knowing how the movie's going to end. Anyway, Mark would go on, you're not truly suicidal. You're just self-destructive. Self-destructive and underachiever are the two most overworked words in America, Grace would yell back, feeling inadequate even to suicide. They'd argue and go to another bar where they'd forget the fight and watch the floor show.

You never knew who you were sitting next to. A drag queen turns out to be a cop, but is such a weirdo you can't believe he's a cop, and then you realize that he's not, he just wants you to think he is. The singer is belting "Heat Wave" and the band has a pretty good horn section, and Grace, in fact, is getting horny, placing her hands on top of her head and wiggling them at Mark, whose attention is elsewhere.

Grace is fascinated with the singer, a young woman with dyed black hair teased as high as the launching pad at Cape Canaveral. Mark grabs the waiter's arm, a young blond man with eyes like a much-used bed. "Tell the singer she's just a kiss away from Hot Shot," he says, looking at Grace. Grace had always had that power: sex.

Alone, Grace is reading "The Black Cat." Ruth would've hated the story. But when Grace read how the main character first gouges out the eye of his faithful cat and then kills it by hanging, a kind of thrill leapt around her body, something like sexual attraction, in a weird way. Another cat just like the first appears and he's missing an eye too. Touching her eyes, Grace turned the page cautiously, as if reading another page might make her blind. Poe was mad, she was sure. She read that he visited Providence toward the end of his life, having lived in Boston, Philadelphia, New York, and Baltimore. He came to Providence to be with a Mrs. Whitman, a poet, sometime after his child bride died. She was thirteen when he married her. Poe's like Jerry Lee Lewis, Grace thought. Mrs. Whitman broke it off twice. That was around 1848. And after she broke it off, he almost married his childhood sweetheart, but on his way to the wedding, one account reported, he got waylaid in Baltimore, did an orgy of drinking, and was found nearly dead in a gutter. They took him to a hospital but he never regained consciousness, so in a sense, he died in the gutter. In Baltimore. I have to go there, Grace thought, Dying in the gutter.

Poe's cruel visions and his symmetrically cruel end relegated Grace's cruelties to conceits. Small potatoes. Potatoes for dinner, when someone fixed them for you. Celia's letter lay on the floor and she picked it up, deciding to answer it, finally.

Dear Celia, I hate writing letters because except for Poe writing seems like the big lie. People can write anything. You should see my mother's letters. What have I been doing? Nothing much. Hanging out in transvestite bars and fucking strangers. I'm a real tramp now. Grace paused. That'll just kill her, she thought.

"If Grace doesn't answer my letters," Ruth announced to her husband, "I won't write her either." Ruth's handwriting was neat, but filled with little flourishes that made her think penmanship class was worth it. The prose was well-formed and affectionate, presenting none of the anger she usually displayed. It was one of those things that Grace hated most about her mother's letters, how phony they were, and bringing one out of her bag, she brandished it at Mark, evidence of treason. "She's trying to be nice," he offered lamely, hating his own mother, feeling he shouldn't. They were at a party given by a much older rich man for his young designer lover. "Designing," Mark hissed. Grace was the only girl. She'd never seen so many men in suits dancing with men in suits. "Think of it as a tableau vivant," Mark went on. Different images do provoke different thoughts. She sat on a crimson velvet love seat and smoked cigarette after cigarette. The white silk curtains were a makeshift screen for porn movies. One of the porn stars, who was supposed to be the postman, looked something like dead President Kennedy, a thought she imagined might be a sin. The host sat down by her side and began a discussion with her on the state of the theater about which she had no opinions, and art films, about which she had some, steering the discussion to horror films, to Hitchcock. They settled on *My Sister, My Love* , a Swedish art house/porn film both had seen and whose incest theme enthralled Grace. Remember the brother and sister lying in bed, almost in state.

What about the scene in the tavern when the old woman lifts her skirt to piss, right there in front of that little boy. The host talked about the film's rustic nature, its sets; Grace slipped, saying flesh for theme. The host used his body as a barrier, practically moving in front of her as he spoke, the porn racing along behind him. From her point of view his bald head looked as if it was in the film, another cast member, or occasionally a bluish image was reflected off it. Later she would think of him as a weird football player. Even though he was trying awfully hard to entertain her, as well as block shots of erections and come shooting into the air, all at the same time, Grace was, against her stubborn will, uncomfortable. She felt invisible. She rose suddenly and said she had to go. He talked her to the door, not allowing her to look back. He kept her hand firmly in his and whispered as she put her coat on, "Let's get together for some good clean fun."

The host didn't know how drawn Grace was to the dark side, the B side, the bad and the beautiful. Early bewitched by Patty McCormack in *The Bad Seed*, while her friends were terrified, Grace saw every scary movie she could, holding her breath and waiting. She wanted more than surprise and hardly ever got really frightened. "Have we got a perpetual inclination, in the teeth of our best judgment, to violate that which is Law, merely because we understand it to be such?...To do wrong for wrong's sake only..." Poe's understanding soothed Grace. That female singer had looked at her. Grace switched the radio on. "I'll do anything that you want me to. I'm your puppet." But in "The Black Cat" the main character does get punished, found out. What's sin without exposure. It's the chance you take. I want to violate the Law, she mugged in her best Bela Lugosi imitation to the mirror that hung near her bed, so that she didn't have to get off the bed to look at herself.

Out the window she could see the tops of houses on Benefit Street. Benefit. Providence. Bringing her knees close to her chin, she raced her fingers through her hair and encircled one breast with her other hand. She struck another pose and looked again into the mirror. She rarely dreamt—remembered them—but lately she'd begun to dream of cats, and it predated the reading of "The Black Cat." It was as if she were reading "The Black Cat" because of her dreams, her cat dreams, the few that stuck. Mark laughed when she recounted how in one there were kittens everywhere, but then it turned weird. Grace's baby is attacked by a small kitten, wounded in the stomach, and while the mother cat tries to kiss the baby, by now the baby is paranoid that it will be attacked again. "Only you," Mark insisted, "could turn kittens into instruments of the devil. My dear, you're the baby."

Celia's letter in return, if Grace were an archivist, which she wasn't, on the contrary, was the kind of document one might keep as evidence of the morals of women in transition in the second half of the twentieth century. Rather than attacking Grace as she'd expected—for being a tramp and a fool—Celia opened up her heart, and it caught Grace entirely by surprise. For one thing Celia wrote that all the time in high school when Grace had flirted at the borders of propriety and then crossed over and Celia hung back or sat on the fence, she had been envious of Grace's courage. Courage was not the word Grace expected. "You're crazy," she answered, "if you call that courage." But Grace liked the idea that she was brave and that it had been courage and not something fashioned from weakness that had driven her so fast and so hard. She didn't look again at what she'd written, sealed it up, jumped into her clothes, and raced outside. It was the tail end of the day. She'd watch *Psycho* again and meet Mark for a drink at a bar where she would look and wait for the rest of the night, looking and waiting were sympathetic activities, similarly requiring her only to be present in the simplest way. And there was a chance of being looked at, which was better than being spoken to: it was as if she were being taken, unaware and involuntarily, and not taken. That other's interest, that gaze on her which felt physical and implied the sexual and left it up to her. Had someone forced himself upon Grace, that would have been another story altogether.

It was a typical night at Oscar's. A few heavy hetero drinkers who looked like small-time gangsters, several drag queens, the singles, the couples, everyone in between. Grace left alone, it was not yet morning, and walked around the good Brown campus where, at dawn, a long, blond man ran wildly through this sedate, plush setting, swinging his arms to chase what turned out to be pigeons. Grace started it by just walking over and staring at him. He was hoping, he told her, to die running. He ran five, six miles a day till his heart banged madly in this thin chest, and he lay panting by the side of the road, smiling. He reminded her of someone who might laugh aloud in his sleep. A true madman, here for her. He talked about death almost immediately. They smoked dope and drove around Providence as people were leaving their houses to go to work. His car veered to the right as he talked and Grace would've jumped out were she not so intent on being brave. She didn't care about dying, anyway.

A list about Bill: studying to be an engineer; loves John Coltrane; wishes he were black; would never fight in Vietnam; intensely political; twenty-one; and a virgin. They would take care of that, Grace surmised, but not right away, she'd nurse it along. She was a good nurse. Let it develop, the way she had developed from good to bad, from a girl without breasts to a girl with breasts. A woman, so-called. You aren't and then you are. You haven't and then you have. Tramp, tramp, tramp, the girls are marching. They go to war. We go to hell. I am a tramp. Which means I'm a poor old man. A loose woman. And someone on the move. It was to Mae West that Cary Grant said, "'When you're bad, you're better." Mark said if he had the choice he'd have been a woman and called himself Norma Bates. Mark didn't like Bill, whose eyes, he sneered, burned like flames from a cheap lighter. Could it be that Mark was jealous? Was that possible? And Grace laughed because there was a way in which it was true, although she spied in Bill's gaze the devotion of a dog, her dog.

But his attentive look was nothing compared with hers at a movie. Nothing comforted her better than sitting through movie after movie, going sometimes early in the day, staying inside until it was dark outside. Grace's guilty pleasures were usually enacted in the dark. Sex, movies, bars, dark pleasure and places where she was inescapably alone. The touch of someone else's skin, another body beside her at the bar, on the bed, or on the floor, not touching this singularity. It began to occur to her in her separation from what she had known—friends, home, neighborhood—that her thoughts, like the physical site, could be shifted, thrown about or thrown out. Why she thought one thing rather than another. Why she liked anyone at all. Why she was heterosexual. Why here rather than there. Europe. Mexico. Colorado. Changing the landscape might change more than the view, her views being, she realized, predicated upon what she had or had not been given, a set of things, facts, conditions over which she had had no control. She had inherited nothing that she wanted to make use of. No, was carrying qualities she had learned like a disease she didn't yet have. If I learned this rather than something else and if I think this rather than that, was taught this not that, does it mean that this and that can't happen? Or won't happen? She dreamt she was in a swimming pool that was a room. It kept filling and she realized she couldn't get out. Just then she saw a cat and a door appeared. Grace told Mark she had stupid dreams.

"Think of me as an animal," she urged Bill. They were in Oscar's listening to her favorite local singer, a man whose voice reminded you, if you closed your eyes, she told Bill, of Smokey Robinson. He said he'd never close his eyes around her. Mark shifted in his seat and grimaced several times but Grace ignored him. Bill was completely in love with her. And frantic to have her. The American government, he was saying, had been lying right along, lying about everything. Grace, wary as she was, had had trust. She had admired JFK, but would never admit to having had heroes, and now it didn't matter anymore. With Bill, she viewed through his devoted eyes a world differently constructed from what she'd been fed. Force-fed, she felt, and was, therefore, very happy to see that world taken apart, as if she could start, in the same way, to take herself apart.

The time came for Bill and Grace to enact a kind of divestiture service in which Bill's virgin state would be renounced, shattered. His virginity existed differently from hers. His was a lack of experience, the sense that he was not really a man, that he was not aggressive enough, not daring, perhaps a coward, or a fag. He had not made a conquest. While hers, she reminded herself, had been a moral burden, something to worry about giving, indicating loss when given. And she was considered to have been a conquest for someone else. A passive gift, whether she moved or not. A given. Surrender and surrender again. But how could something physically surrendered mean that she, Grace, had really given in. She prided herself on her ability to separate neatly body from mind, self that was hers from self that she gave away. She was not given when she gave, she always held back and drew satisfaction from distance.

The night Bill brought her back to his room, she took her place in the center of it, feeling very certain that she would make the conquest, she would take it from him. He turned on the record player and she undressed. He lay his head on her breast and kissed the nipple many times, licking it like her dog would've, she thought, and she waited for him to make the move. For his penis to become erect the way every penis she'd ever encountered had. He rubbed himself against her and she moved her hand, down there, and Bill caught it and held it, not letting Grace, the way she hadn't let boys when she used to stop them. Engaging in a wordless struggle, Grace moved more violently to grip his cock, which lay there small and soft and malleable. Impotence became dangerous. The room looked ugly. His penis was useless and its absence felt like an attack. And then he cried that he did really love her. Fear turns quickly to disgust. Why hadn't Poe ever written about impotence? Or was it there somehow, disguised in the terror? Look for castration, Mark pounced, that's what you'll find, if you look hard enough. Or soft, he laughed. But soft? What light through yonder window breaks...

Dear Celia, I have a boyfriend who can't get it up, so I'm going to stop seeing him, because I can't stand it. It's too weird. He always cries and says that he loves me, but I can't help him and it drives me crazy and I don't want...I mean, I want. Grace tore the letter up and went looking for what she might determine later was trouble.

Chapter 5

There is nothing to fear but fear itself, Emily mused as she put on her clothes. The cheap record player, which she turned on the moment she turned off her alarm clock, having punched the snooze alarm five times, got stuck on that part in "Baby Love" where it goes "breaking up...making up..." It's better never to have reasoned than to have reasoned badly. She wanted to conduct her life through the mail. The phone was ringing in its insistent way. She knew it would be Christine, needing her help with something or other. Okay, Emily said, I'll be over soon. Breaking up with Richard had happened at a distance, through letters, so perhaps she shouldn't trust her personal life to the vagaries of correspondence. Their breakup was civilized, she supposed someone might say that about it, and while she liked the notion in an abstract way, the idea was better suited to English movies celebrating WW II that came on at 3 A.M.

Lying on Edith's bed, the television on, Emily was explaining to Edith what had happened in art class. While she didn't consider herself an artist, or consider that she might become one, Emily liked to draw and to paint. It's a different way of thinking, she continued during the commercial. She told Edith that the handsome male drawing teacher—there were no women teachers in the art department—had asked the class to copy two drawings of interiors from their Janson *History of Art* book. I copied one of a room, I forget who did it, and the other one I chose was by Leonardo, of a fetus in a womb. When I showed them to my teacher he stared at the womb one for a while, and then he gave me a look. He said, "I said interior." I said, this is an interior. He didn't say anything for a minute and then he said, "When you're an old woman, you're going to be very eccentric." Emily laughed as she told Edith. Edith took another cracker and didn't speak. The commercial ended and the movie came back on. Emily was supposed to be reading seventeenth-century poetry for her 8 A.M. class and Edith should have been reading her friend's book on raising children, though he hadn't, a fact that Emily held against him. Young people could be such purists, Edith thought—the womb as an interior. It made her smile inwardly. She liked being around young Emily, but she was happy not to be young, a feeling that she thought she'd never have, having heard about it years before, when she was young. Is this the way the body prepares for death, she thought as she rubbed hand cream on her fingers and economically patted the excess on both elbows.

Christine phoned Emily. Emily went right over. He's violent, she reported of Peter, her Slavic lover, as she called him. To Christine, Slavic itself implied violence, or if not real violence, then excitement and volatility, terms very different from those with which she described herself. Just one of the few poor whites from Westchester. "What do you mean, violent?" Emily asked. "Did he hit you?" Christine showed Emily the bruises on the upper part of her body. "I'm afraid of him," Christine said. "Of course you are," Emily reassured her, "he's crazy," Christine had already lived with a man, though the two young women were only nineteen, and because they were only nineteen and Emily a young nineteen, Edith told her, it seemed a mark of great maturity to have already lived with a man, a man ten years older, too, who was a sculptor. But then, considered Emily, Christine had lost her father when she was eleven, and he had been a painter, and so it made sense that she would quickly live with a man. At nineteen things seem very simple. "You don't know what this is like," Christine continued. "I'm afraid of what he'll do." "Can't you stop seeing him?" Emily asked sensibly, pouring herself a glass of wine, drinking and pulling at single strands of her hair. "You don't understand," Christine uttered in a kind of moan, and looked at Emily as if she were just a visitor. "I guess I don't," Emily responded. And she didn't. Was she going to cry, thought Emily, at a loss, desperate to return to her small room and read. Christine often chided Emily for wanting to avoid life. I have plenty of time for that, Emily thought as she walked home from Christine's apartment which was only five houses from hers, closer even than Nora's had been. Is proximity the best basis for a friendship, she wondered.

Her parents said she didn't call them enough or visit them enough. It wasn't normal, they said. Emily had a hard time remembering she had parents; they weren't in the picture, as no one from her former life, as she liked to put it, was, as if she had led a dangerous one. While she had been fastidious in high school, Emily lost all concern for what she looked like, she said. The tyranny of changing clothes, of wearing something different each day to school, was overthrown. It's not exactly criminal, Edith thought, although that very phrase did come to mind; she was sure that Emily could be such a pretty girl, if she wanted to. She didn't say this to Emily; she would of course have said that to her own daughter.

Christine was to do battle with Peter one night and Edith and Emily took in a movie, Buñuel's *The Exterminating Angel*. Christine never minded if Emily went out with Edith, because Edith was so much older, but she bristled when Emily wanted to see any of her other friends, and gradually Emily stopped seeing them. She spoke to them on the phone. Edith said nothing about this either. They didn't go out together often, but Edith especially enjoyed it when they did, especially because Emily could have been her daughter and wasn't, a fact which meant more to her than she thought it should. She felt a certain irresponsibility, almost collusion with her young tenant. She felt they made a bizarre pair and when they bumped into people Edith knew, she introduced Emily proudly, as my tenant, the poet or the student, a young person who was visibly different from people she had known for thirty years. She wondered if her husband would understand this enjoyment and decided he would. Emily was struck by *The Exterminating Angel*, figuring it had to do with neurosis in general, and that maybe she too couldn't leave her room in the way that Buñuel meant. You think there's something out there and there isn't, except for what you think is there stopping you. She turned to Edith as they entered the dark apartment and quoted Kafka. "My education has damaged me in ways I do not even know." Edith argued briefly, defending the necessity of education, then let it go, glad that she didn't think about Kafka anymore, and never had just before bed.

Emily wrote a poem about receiving and sending letters that was so romantic it surprised her. She was aware of this tendency in herself, but it was usually mixed like a salad dressing with a lot of other tendencies and wasn't so naked. The naked truth: the oil separates from the vinegar. She laughed and shoved it into the drawer she optimistically called To Be Published, and shut it. She never showed her work to anyone, although she didn't consider herself a secret writer. She said she wasn't ready and squirreled her poems away, keeping them to herself, even keeping them from Christine. It was another thing they fought about. You're not a writer, Christine intoned, if your work sits in a drawer and no one sees it. When it's ready I'll show it, Emily would respond, as if her drawer were an oven in which her poems were baking. Christine and Emily fought and made up, fought and made up. Generally, they fought about intangibles, the ineffable. When Emily realized that she hadn't seen one of her very closest friends in nearly a year, she startled, called her, and made a date. Christine acted like a lover betrayed. Emily went anyway. You don't have to obey her, her other friend told her. I don't understand what she wants from me, Emily added, to which her friend countered, What do you want from her?

Are we lesbians and we don't know it, Emily deliberated when walking home, walking fast to speed up her thoughts. Her mind sorted things back and forth, a shovel digging up stuff and separating it into discrete piles. Except nothing was discrete. She'd been too demanding. On the other hand, I can't stand it when she disappears for weeks with a new guy. That means I'm possessive about her too. She felt as if she were in a cave and she had always hated the dark. She visualized herself: a child, lying in bed, the blanket up to her eyes, no light in the hall, no light anywhere. What bothered her most was that there was no way to determine right and wrong, or to determine if those categories applied to relationships. She supposed that this was what was meant by mystery. They made up, they made up as they always did. They spent as much time as they could together.

Movies, bars, school. They went to see *Persona*. When the two actress-es' heads merged, Emily screamed. Several people turned to look at her. You're so emotional, Christine teased. Me? Emily asked, defen-sively, deciding in her mind that poets should be, a thought she kept to herself hopefully.

For Emily was hopeful, it was astonishing how much hope she had, Edith reflected as she washed the dishes, carefully drying the paper towels though she knew Emily thought that was cheap. Emily hadn't grown up during the Depression. Edith always thought that thought and sometimes decided that that thought might be too convenient for all the questions it was supposed to answer. Well, it certainly was a part of it, she continued to herself as she put each dish away in the yellow cupboard. This was a rent-controlled apart-ment and she blessed the day she'd moved in, a young woman, with a husband and two small children, over twenty years ago. Finding herself staring at the cupboard, she shut it, conscious that the way her arm moved now was the way it moved then. She was never going to move. She could be very stubborn; her husband could have attested to that. And her children. "They'll have to take me away," she had said to her husband, who had been a sociologist. "You can't stop change, Edith," he had answered. "I'm not stopping it, I'm just not going to be a party to it." Then, she remembered, he'd touched her on the arm and laughed. He had such a wonderful laugh, Edith thought, and left the kitchen.

"Makeup"—Christine smiled—"makes some of my imperfec-tions more obvious. More perfect." They had just eaten an enor-mous bowl of salad and tuna fish. "I like you without makeup," said Emily, who wore less of it, or none. Emily was considering letting her eyebrows grow in. First, she thought she looked too much like Bette Davis playing Queen Elizabeth. Second, they looked like parentheses on her forehead. "I look like a clown." "Of course you don't," Christine insisted. "Your face is perfect." They smiled at each other over the big bowl. "Dare I eat a peach or wear my trousers rolled?" Emily mimicked. Christine smiled again, encouragingly—Emily had had a man over the night before—"let them grow," she urged, as if growing one's eyebrows signified activity.

It was Valentine's Day, a fact the two young women noted, cynically, over the tuna fish, mentioning having received valentines when they were young, in grade school, Emily remembering her love for Peter. Dressing up. Kissing games. My mother taught me never to lie. She'd received this day a card from Richard, who was in Italy, driving around the hill towns. With someone, probably, she commented to Christine. Emily did not want to talk about last night. It was disappointing. Oddly enough, Edith had had a man over the night before too. Emily had gone in the back door—the maid's entrance—and Edith had used the front one, as she always did, so, in a sense, they had missed each other. Emily heard a man's voice in the morning. Edith saw a cigarette on her dining-room table. Both were made aware, but neither spoke of it. It was something they didn't enter into with each other. Emily would never discuss sex with Edith, that was reserved for Christine. The subject with Edith was skirted; she amused herself with the image. We pull in our skirts so as not to appear like flirts. Emily never wore skirts anyway, which her mother found difficult to digest, like Mexican food. "And she always wears the same things," she complained to her husband. "Those army pants that are falling apart. And she never tells us about her boyfriends. If she has them."

Her parents couldn't decide which was worse—her having them or not having them. Emily's father threw up his hands like an evangelist enlisting God's aid. "It's not normal," he said. Both parents shook their heads in unison.

"My mother walked right out of the room when I walked in." Emily was reporting to Edith about her latest visit with her parents. "She couldn't stand the way I looked." Emily started to cry then stopped, suddenly, just turning it off. A leaky faucet in Edith's bathroom appeared like a cartoon in the older woman's mind. She didn't want to be emotionally involved, she kept telling herself, using those exact words. I do not want to be emotionally involved. The two women walked into Central Park and sat on a large grey boulder that stuck up from the ground, a tough couch for Emily's sorrows. That's how life is, Edith kept thinking, she'll get used to it. Edith restrained herself from saying that your mother can't help it. She had parents too. But she didn't say it because she didn't want to be an apologist for parents. Stretched before her she saw long lines of children and their parents and then their parents and their parents. "It must have been awful at the very beginning of time," she said, ending her vision. "I'm just thinking out loud," she told Emily.

They watched walkers and bikers and runners. They stayed for three hours. A civil rights march that had begun in Harlem passed right in front of them. In fact, it stopped in front of them, allowing Nelson Rockefeller to get out of his black limo and join its ranks. He walked by them; he was so close they could have slapped him on the back. Rockefeller forced himself between two black men in the front line whose arms were tight around each other's backs. Their arms relaxed truculently, and he took his place between them, as if he were born to be there. Emily was astonished at his lack of feelings, maybe it wasn't a lack of feelings. She was astonished at his wanting to get his own way and knowing that he could and would. She concluded that a great fortune makes people indifferent, imperious. He had acted like an emperor. Emily had nearly forgotten about her mother by the time she opened the door to her small room. The phone rang. Her mother said, "I didn't realize I could hurt your feelings."

As for Edith, it was Sunday, and on Sunday she did not want to think about her children and their feelings. She wanted to read *The New York Times* and make herself a sandwich. That night Christine's mother called her daughter. She called faithfully every Sunday. "Your father left me nothing. I'll have to work for the rest of my life in a dentist's office," recited tonight exactly as it had been done over the years, and responded to by Christine with the same precision. Mixed with the complaints was a sense of the absurd, the absurdity of their situation, mother and daughter, together, against the world, a sensibility that Christine comprehended and inherited, so to speak, rather than money.

Emily never worried about money; they had always had enough and her father wasn't dead. It irritated but also pleased Christine to be close with someone who didn't care night and day, day and night, about how she was going to survive. Emily never seemed to think about it. She's not very realistic, thought Christine, who was herself practical and wary, not the optimist Emily was, not by a long shot. She explained to Emily that she had become a fatalist at an early age. But somewhere Christine comforted herself with the belief that life, like the end of a fairy tale, would present her with a happy ending, a man to support her. It was a belief deep inside her, but being practical she set about to become financially independent. The fantasy was a bas-relief, lifting her slightly above everyday exigencies. It was another thing that Emily didn't really understand about Christine, this dread of poverty, fueling her friend into action more often than Emily would ever realize.

Still later, Edith read into the night, restless with denial; Christine decided again never to see Peter; and, having buried her mother's phone call into ground that is not conscious, Emily worked on a poem that began:

Leo strides in a field of men like a motorcycle passing cars. She is too different to be used yet. The cat wears its coat mindless of any beauty because beauty is only a word.

Tired and not tired, Emily stopped writing and placed the piece of paper in the drawer, turned off the light, and stared ahead into the dark space that was not completely black. There was light coming from a small window in her bathroom. She always kept the bathroom door open, to let that little bit of light in.

Chapter 6

"You shouldn't listen to your sisters, Jane, they overpower you." The woman who said this was undressing as she spoke. She was showing the younger woman how to undress on the beach, European style. "You hold your towel like this, then you quietly tug at your pants." Jane wanted to say that she was never even able to open *The New York Times* the right way on the train, but skipped it, thinking the Hungarian woman wouldn't get it, and said instead, "I didn't bring my bathing suit anyway." She was back up the scale again. She would never get undressed on the beach, but she didn't tell Sinuway that.

They had taken the subway to a Brooklyn beach that Sinuway went to often. The Hungarian woman had had a sister who died during the 1956 uprising. She told Jane, "You are lovely too, so was my sister, exquisite," then gave Jane a small round mirror with odd markings on the back which she said Jane was to look into to know that she was a fine woman. Jane thought Sinuway was talking out of a novel. She had, though, gotten all her clothes off without any skin showing. The older woman said many things that the younger one listened to but would not hear until years later, and then like an echo.

Sinuway had wild, coarse red hair, perhaps all her features were coarse, and to Jane she was both plain and exotic, living in a tiny apartment on St. Mark's Place, speaking from experience about the world. She said she was going to marry a professor but Jane never met him. It was conceivable that he didn't exist, or that he was part of Sinuway's book, or her mind, so foreign to Jane.

Despite the meaning of her name, "one who walks alone," Sinuway gathered people to her. Besides Jane there was Carl and occasionally Jimmy, Jane's childhood love. Carl lived across the street from Sinuway and was crippled. He had an angel's face, thin and dark, like a study by Leonardo, Sinuway would say, and his legs dragged behind him. Jane wanted to be in love with Carl because he was crippled; she wanted to be able to be in love with him, but she wasn't.

Jane passed time with the Hungarian woman and Carl. "Let's go to a castle," Sinuway exclaimed. "Where?" "In New Jersey." "There's a castle in New Jersey?" "Would I say let's go to a castle if there wasn't a castle? Are you thinking I'm crazy, Jane?" Jane was always thinking everyone was crazy. "No, let's go. What do you think, Carl?" Carl had a small white car specially built for him. The three of them just fit into it, Jane sitting on the ledge, Sinuway getting the guest of honor's seat, as she called it, "because I'm the oldest." As the youngest in her family, Jane never expected to become the oldest anywhere. "You have much to learn, little one," Sinuway said, annoying Jane. Still, when Sinuway spoke in her accented English, every syllable had more meaning.

There's a castle in New Jersey. The three arrived there late one evening. A wealthy American in the beginning of this century, Sinuway reported, had a Scottish castle shipped to New Jersey, stone by stone. "Americans want to be cultured so they bring Europe here, by boat," she said. They walked from room to room. The air inside was damp, and Jane can't remember how they got in, although she is almost positive it was entirely legal. Sinuway must have known someone. All three of them felt awkward in the castle, riding to it had been more fun.

Later, in the car, Sinuway talked more about transplanting cultures, which sounded to Jane like discussing a yeast infection. "I myself am a transplant," Sinuway said. "I will never fit here, in America. It is not possible."

Jane came to believe that what Sinuway said was something akin to Hungarian folk philosophy, none of which she could repeat word for word, the words being spoken huskily into the wind as they drove back to Manhattan, or as they sat in a small room. "There is a castle in Spoleto called La Rocca," she told Carl and Jane, "that was started in the fourteenth century and finished in the middle of the fifteenth by Pope Nicholas the Fifth. It was used as the residence for papal governors. But today it is a prison. So you see it is crazy to transplant things because there is a place for them and that place changes but people don't know that if they are not there and they worship the wrong things. Who cares about an old castle?" Sinuway looked at Carl, who said, "It was your idea to come here." "Yes, I know," she said, "I wanted you to see it for yourself." Even the way Sinuway said "see" was different. It sounded like what it meant. "And where is Jimmy tonight?" she asked Jane. "I don't know," Jane answered, thinking he's probably getting high somewhere in the city.

Somewhere in the city Jimmy was taking some grass out of a child's plastic beach pail that was kept under his dealer and friend's couch. He started laughing and laughing, his crooked teeth set so strangely in his mouth, sticking out like tiny marshmallows, or so they looked to his friend. "Your teeth look ugly enough to eat, man," his friend said. "Where's your suburban girlfriend on a wet night like this?" Jimmy breathed in and out and felt his heart which was still beating. "How would I know. And she's not my girlfriend," Jimmy said. "She's a pain in the ass." "She's great, Jimmy," his friend laughed. "A little on the naive side. But she's great." "She's all right. She got a little too much when she was taking speed," Jimmy yawned. "Now she's just a little too much on the weight side." "Maybe she's always too much," his friend said. "Not for me," Jimmy said, not thinking it over.

"Why do you hang around with Jimmy if it makes you feel so awful?" Sinuway asked. "It doesn't," Jane said. The next night she was in Jimmy's antique store, the one he owned with an older man, a lover of men, Sinuway called him. Maurice always gave Jane dirty looks, but tonight he gave her especially dirty looks because he was tripping. Jane was a freshman in college, and Maurice hated college girls. Jane was sitting on the floor, reading, and Maurice was staring at a vase and talking about *The Golden Bow*, which Jane had not read. Upon hearing that Jane had not read James's classic, Maurice swelled, his face becoming a bright red, and he attempted to tear her apart with language. Felix, Jimmy's Swiss painter friend, walked in just as Maurice was reaching his climax: "Stupid college girls in pea jackets." Felix grabbed Jane's hand, told Maurice to shut up, and they walked out.

"Let's go for coffee. You shouldn't listen to that shit, Jane," Felix said. "He's in love with Jimmy and he hates it every time you walk into that shitty antique store." Felix enjoyed saying shit. They'd met a couple of times, but they'd never talked. "Jimmy's an old friend," Jane said, "it's not like that between us." Felix whooped, or so it sounded to Jane. "Jimmy's a weird guy, you know. You may have come from the same town, but that's shit." Jane wondered why she'd never really looked at Felix before, while he grew to look more and more like Sinuway though he was skinny and tall, and Sinuway broad and short. Jane was uneasy with him. He announced unexpectedly, "I like you. Has Jimmy ever told you that?" Jane just looked at him. "You can visit me sometimes, I don't ask anyone, and if I'm busy I'll tell you. No shit, okay?" Jane said okay, and took the bus home.

Sinuway disappeared. She said she was going to leave and she did; all along it had been inevitable, Jane thought, and I didn't take her seriously, Sinuway left no clues to her whereabouts and even Carl knew nothing about what had happened to her, or if she had gotten married to the professor no one had ever met, or what. Carl and Jane spent some desultory evenings drinking weak coffee in restaurants. Their connection was altered, then broken, by Sinuway's absence. It was as if there had been nothing between them at all. After a while they drifted out of each other's lives, the parting having no particular shape. Jane was used to absence and disappearance, her sisters' boyfriends coming and going. Lois going. It was like Sinuway was dead and all that was left was the mirror she'd given Jane.

"You're perfect," Felix told Jane, as they ate a cheap breakfast on First Avenue New Year's morning, "you're perfect except for sex." Jane made no claims on Felix, which he attributed to her being a virgin and fucked-up, the way he thought all American girls from the suburbs were. She'd visit his studio and sit in the corner, read a magazine or something from school, then leave without saying when she'd be back. Sometimes he'd want her to pose for him, because he couldn't afford models, but she wouldn't want to pose in the nude. He'd rant and rave in his funny accent and she'd undress halfway, the way

Dorothy Parker walked out halfway when Alexander Woollcott told an anti-Semitic joke because she was half Jewish. Felix would paint for a while, then slam down his brushes, demanding total nudity. Jane would walk out, fast and silent. Then Felix would run after her and tell her she was right, he had no right to demand anything of her that she didn't want to do.

Jimmy was running an avant-garde movie house, the antique store having gone bust, but Maurice was still in the picture as were Jimmy's parents, who supported all his projects. Jane met Jimmy's mother on the LIRR one day when she was returning from an infrequent visit with her parents. His mother quizzed her about Jimmy, as if Jane knew a secret that everyone knew but his parents. They wanted to know about Maurice. "Jimmy's always liked you, Jane," the mother said too evenly. Then she looked into Jane's eyes and said, "Young people have to experience things their own way. I'm sure Jimmy will be all right, aren't you?" Jane said she was certain Jimmy would be all right, as if she was agreeing about his getting over an illness she wasn't sure he had or if he had it, was it a disease? But she was forced to comfort Jimmy's mother for, though she appeared composed in her elegant going-to-the-city suit, everything was so close to the surface, it looked like her makeup might crack up and fall off and her tailored clothes come apart at the seams. Jane didn't tell Jimmy that she had seen his mother. Later she cooked him too much spaghetti and they got stoned. Then they went to his theater, where he was showing a French film about slaughterhouses, and Jane left after the first scene when the butcher hit the horse on the head and the horse's legs went out from under him and he was dead.

77

Perfect except for sex, Felix was thinking. He got undressed and placed his cock in her small hands and said, "For you, Jane," and his cock lay rigid in a grip that barely held it and then only for a little while. "No one will ever do this with you, the way I'm doing," he said. "We'll do whatever you want." "I don't want to do anything," Jane said. She was remembering that the last time she was with Jimmy he said to her, "You want to make love with me, don't you?" But he said it as if it were a dare and Jane didn't feel daring. "You're always thinking about Jimmy," Felix said. "I can tell by that shitty look you get on your face." "Let's go see a movie and eat some chocolate," Jane answered. "Oh, your hips—Jane—oh, your diet. I love your hips." Europeans were great to be around, Jane thought, if you're fat. They think you're like a Rubens or a Renoir, just a happy voluptuary. Then he looked at her, so determined, and said, "Okay, let's go to a movie," and he put his clothes back on.

It went like that the winter after Sinuway left. When Jane imagined Sinuway alive, she imagined her living in a different part of the city, like the Upper West Side, with or without the professor she did or did not marry. There were echoes everywhere. She wrote in her diary: Something remembered is invisible. What did I think about BEFORE, when I was young? I'm part of what I was thinking about then but it's not there anymore. The sum of my parts is invisible. Jane liked that line, "sum of my parts," a person could be added to or subtracted from, or a person could add up to anything. Or not. "She didn't amount to much." "It didn't amount to much."

The doorbell rang unexpectedly. She was thinking, in the shower, and nearly didn't respond. Throwing on a robe, she asked who it was and she heard him say: Your father. She opened the door partway, and said she couldn't talk, that she was late. Only later did she realize that she hadn't taken the chain lock off the door.

She thought about Lois the way some people keep Holden Caulfield in mind, to check their humanity, to see if they're still young. Jimmy teased her about her passion to remember, while other people, he told her, have a passion to forget. "It's almost a mission for some people—to forget." He said this to her while she studied Spinoza, on speed. He was looking at imperceptible progress. The sister she shared the apartment with was out of town, and Jimmy could stay all night if he wanted. She wanted him to. Jimmy stared at her as she read and she found it comforting. "What do you think of Spinoza?" he asked as she was leaving for school. "I think it doesn't matter what I think. Either I'm crazy or everything is going in circles." "That's philosophy. You're not crazy." Her legs began to shake. She hadn't taken much speed since she'd kicked the habit, in a manner of speaking, because she wouldn't have put it that way, then. The subway ride was hell. By the time she got to class, and was handed the test by the sincere Catholic poet/philosopher who led the class, and thought on his feet in front of them like a performing seal trained to wonder why, she could barely remember anything. Mr. Arnold walked over to her and suggested she start writing. She looked at him, benignly, and something snapped so that she lifted her ballpoint pen and her hand began moving as if she were doing automatic writing. "You shouldn't do speed at all," Jimmy said. "You're one to talk," Jane said. He said he could handle it and that he didn't have to take tests about Spinoza. Jane thought about dropping out.

Felix was in one of his high German moods, or so Jane put it. His girlfriend was coming back from Spain. Jane herself was nonplussed, not being, in her mind, anything like a girlfriend. "I'll handle it," he told her. "What's there to handle?" she answered. "Let's go see a movie at the museum." Felix was looking at his foot and muttering to himself. "This is boring," Jane protested. "It's raining, you're looking at your foot, I have to read some stuff I don't want to…" "And…?" Felix asked. "And nothing."

There were a few, maybe twenty more minutes of this kind of nothing that occurs between people who spend a great deal of time together and probably shouldn't. "It's all dead in here," Felix nearly shouted as they went around on the second floor—the permanent collection—of the museum. "Dead." There's nothing permanent was his modernist point, a point not at all lost on Jane, the way Felix considered sex was. Felix railed against museums, it was still raining, Jane was barely listening, and they went into the museum's auditorium to watch some Bruce Conner films. "The first time I ever came to see a movie here I was with Jimmy," Jane whispered as the lights went down. Felix sank deeper into his seat and lit a cigarette. They were kicked out right after. "See those uniforms those men—those doormen—wear, look at those guys, Jane." "I don't want to look at uniforms. Stop trying to distract me from being pissed off at you, you asshole." Felix walked defiantly up to one of the Plaza doormen and started a conversation with him. In German, as the doorman had come not so long ago from Berlin and worked in a large hotel there. He told Felix that rich people were the same the world over.

That anyway was what Felix told Jane the doorman said, but Jane withheld belief. "You never really believe me," Felix told her, "I can feel that and it's because you're from the suburbs of this shitty country." "And where are you from—Switzerland—a bunch of mountains, some chocolate, and a clock. A lot of clocks. You think being an artist isn't middle class?" was Jane's final rejoinder. They went downtown silently together. She got off before him and went back to her apartment. He continued for a few more stops and went to his storefront and there she was, his girlfriend Andrea back from Spain. It was nearly the end of winter, that's why it was raining so much.

Jane hated spring, when the air smelled so alive and people took off their coats and their figures showed. Spring and summer, the terrible times to be fat. "You're not fat, Jane, you're overweight." Her Uncle Larry was the only one she allowed to tease her. He was even fatter but he was fun. "Bugsy Seigel wasn't going to allow the syndicate to build another hotel in Vegas unless they bailed him out. He was going to squeal. They got him on a train," Larry went on. He'd told her the story before but it didn't matter. "Hemingway was a bum. We fished together around Cuba. Think I'm fat. He never stopped drinking." They were driving around Manhattan in Larry's convertible, a pale yellow Buick with a white top. "And what about sex? I won't tell your father," he said and puffed on his cigar. "There's nothing to tell, Uncle Larry. I think I'm in love with someone who's not in love with me and someone who likes me—that way—it never even occurs to me," Jane said and looked at the Flatiron Building, with its funny triangular shape. "The whole family's crazy," Larry said. "No reason you should be an exception but listen to me, kid. Try to have a good time. I'm just learning that. There's not too much else. Have a few laughs." The sun was setting as he drove her back to her apartment. The air was heavy with nostalgia. "Take it easy," he said at her door. "Look at your father—he worries night and day—and where does it get him. There's no percentage in worrying." Larry still played the horses even though business was worse than ever. "You've gotta have some fun in life, right?" Jane hated spring.

Part III

Mark read aloud from his notebook: "Once I was in a sentimental hospital. The nurse's uniform was starched, and her hands soft, the fingers wrinkled, as if she'd been in the bathtub all day long. When I cried out, she heard me, rushing to my bedside, a line of concern etched into her noble brow. A hand quickly laid on my feverish forehead, she soothed me and restored my soul…" Mark repeated "my soul" and faltered. "They talked about the soul."

Mark dangled, like a pendulum, over sentimentality and cynicism, his direction changing, reflecting a kind of weather. While he was sensitive, it was a sensitivity not unlike that experienced under laughing gas. You're numb and don't care about anything and you don't know if you're able to control your facial muscles or not. When pain comes, in this indifferent state, it is bad, worse, because you have been lulled into a kind of inviolability, Mark's favorite word, next to epicene. Most of the time you don't feel anything, as if encased by a prophylactic. All this led him to the Pre-Raphaelites. He told Grace that pubic hair was absent from their paintings of nude women, that it was discovered later, that all the hair was on top, mounds and mounds of it. Grace slid off the barstool and walked to the jukebox, where she watched the record turn. Mark was rejected by some men because they were straight, he rejected others because they were too serious, and some rejected him because he was too much of a woman, or not enough of one. "I'm a displaced person, a country without a man. A guest in my own body." "You have beautiful eyes," Grace told him. "The doorway to the ignored soul," he muttered. His Bible, his comfort, was "Notes on Camp," which he insisted Grace read as a way to know him. He told her some people would call her a fag hag. She said, "They can go fuck themselves." He said, "I love you when you're brutal."

Silence Is Golden hung over the sink in Ruth's kitchen, its yellow walls and shelves, its linoleum floor; her domain. It was the room from which she wrote Grace those occasional letters, during which time she glanced every now and then at the sign above the sink, which restored to her something that might have been lost for a moment or two. Smoothing her housedress under her as she sat down at the circular table, chosen because you could fit more people around it and it meant harmony, she took out her letter paper with her name at its top, her married name she always added silently, and touched the raised letters. Dear Grace, Your father and I worry that…The coffee maker gurgled, and Ruth walked over to the pot, reminding herself of that woman in the TV commercial. Why did that woman wear pearls around her neck when she was washing the dishes? Ruth touched her bare skin, where a necklace could have been, and felt sensible.

On a cold Providence morning Bill ran around the campus, lonely for Grace. She hadn't called him in two weeks and the last time she saw him she told him she couldn't handle his problem. In the distance two shapes were clinging to each other, and as if life weren't bad enough, it was Grace sticking her tongue into some guy's mouth he'd never seen before, and she probably hadn't either. Look at that. Bill ran in the opposite direction to a diner where he ordered a cup of coffee and saw nothing. Blind, he drank it and asked himself why God would bother with such petty details like his heart when there were wars, famines, tornadoes that needed attention. He thought about what going off to war would do at a moment like this, and wished he felt like dying for his country or being a mercenary instead of sitting around bleeding for what might appear to anyone as no reason. A girl.

Dear G,

I saw you with him, and knew you had lied to me. We can never be friends. We were friends for weeks and then came that night, my night, and it didn't work. Did you ever think I was scared or nervous? Did you ever think you were tight? My problem, but your problem too. I was there for you but you weren't there for me. No one had ever been there for you. I know that. I feel the way I felt after Coltrane died except you wouldn't understand that because you don't feel... You're like every other white person in this country—dead. You don't feel, do you know that? You don't dig men, you only dig men who are half female. "White women become men things, a weird combination, sucking the male juices to build a navel orange, which is themselves."—LeRoi Jones. I'm even sensitive enough to realize you don't love me or never did. Maybe I'll kill myself, maybe I won't. I wanted to prove myself to you. And you're nothing. I'll always love you. I hate you.

Bill

This letter was followed by an apology that told her no one would ever teach him as much or would ever be as cool. Mark couldn't get over women's being compared with a navel orange, and elaborated on the fag-hag stuff. Grace felt little or nothing beyond the initial shock of receiving it, it being in black and white, and even enjoyed the letter because it was honest. People don't talk like that. It's like Poe. "You're becoming more literary every day," Mark said, and she told him to go to hell.

Grace had cut off from Bill the way her mother used to cut away material when sewing from a pattern. The big scissors bearing down, her mother's hand steady, discarding without a second look. The revulsion had turned into disinterest. She couldn't explain to Mark how Bill's impotence caused her to feel. Trapped with him in a kind of void, and then maybe they'd disappear together. It was as if she were that soft penis and how could she tell Mark that. She laughed out loud, to herself, watching the R & B band.

"The Telltale Heart" is just like "The Black Cat" except it's an old man who the main character thinks has the evil eye. Maybe Poe thought the eye was the soul, too, the way Mark does, and that it could look right into every evil part of him. Mark had given Grace a cross that lay on the table next to her bed. On its back were the words Faith and Grace, Faith vertical and Grace horizontal, both sharing the letter A. That was the scarlet letter, he said, when he handed it to her. Killing his wife was a mistake that makes the story more horrible. But what got Grace about both stories was that suddenly a man wants to kill something that he loves. Just like that. Out of nowhere. You can understand something, somewhere deep inside you, but you can't say what you understand and what you don't understand. It's as if the killing substitutes for not being able to understand. In the story. And for the person who's reading the story. It's weird. They never get away with it and you know that they'd do it again, because even if they knew they'd be caught, they can't help themselves. They're helpless. Slaves.

Grace didn't want to appear slavish. There was playing with fire and there was getting burned. She might be slavish to desire, but that was her desire. There were slaves and there were slaves. Her private life was her business. She owned it like a coat or a record. She imagined a sign on an office door that read Fantasy—My Business, and she'd be a kind of detective operating a lost-and-found…What she thought about when she stared out a window or rode on a bus or looked in a mirror over a bar, that was hers. Or that was hers, that momentary sensation. In a way, she thought, it was all anybody ever really had.

The Epicene Is Everything was written in pink nail polish on the frame around Mark's bathroom mirror. Gay is better than homosexual as a word, he thought, because homosexual sounds so single-minded. "On the other hand, when I say I'm gay, I feel I have to be happy." Grace washed the dishes and Mark stood behind her, speaking to her back. He said he'd fallen in love with a boy with long brown wavy hair. The feeling had extended beyond their first date, as he put it, and the boy—he was only three years younger than Mark, but Mark felt ancient—had moved in. Grace interrupted. "The plots are nearly identical. Then I read that Poe said the most perfect subject for a poem was a dead woman or the death of a beautiful woman, I forget which." "My photographs are always the same," Mark said, "you walk down the street the same way." "But if you're going to write a story why would you write the same story again and again." "Maybe you'll finally get it right. Or, maybe you like the story better than anything else."

Mark had given her an old movie poster. Born to Be Bad. To Be Kissed. *Human Desire*, the movie's title, written in even bigger letters. The poster hung over her bed. Advertising, Mark asked. It was funny, she knew it seemed like that, like the Rolling Stones were like that, teasing and very aware of it. Probably laughing at all of them. Us. If someone wants to believe the words, let them. They're only words. She preferred to announce it, to say it before it was said. Throw it at them. Not that you send engraved invitations saying Strange But She Doesn't Care. But if you did, they'd probably love it. Usually it's just a song and no one lives up to it. She answered Celia's letter, telling her about the poster, and Mark's new boyfriend and how she worried that she wouldn't see him as much, and Celia answered the letter, the way she always did, but couldn't answer the questions that weren't written. Grace fumed over a Velvet Underground album and put the needle down on "All Tomorrow's Parties."

There was a new patient in the mental hospital, a sixteen-year-old named Ellen. Ellen told Grace she was an octoroon, but it turned out that her mother was white and her father black and years ago when she was two she'd been taken by her mother's family and placed for adoption, because they said her mother couldn't take care of her, she was no more than a child herself. Which was true, she was a child, but it wasn't that. "She loved me," Ellen cried, "I know that. She gave me this," and pointed to a battered teddy bear. Then she put her cigarette out in its stomach. Sometimes Ellen didn't seem crazy at all. She just didn't have a real home and now she couldn't take care of herself, all those foster homes, and no one teaching her anything. Next to Ellen, Grace felt accomplished. Ellen would never age in a nuthouse. If she were just a little more in touch, Grace thought they could have been friends, remembering her mother's admonition that it was more difficult to make friends when you got older. It was said the summer that "Good Vibrations" came out and everyone in high school was saying that Brian Wilson was a genius. Good, good, good, good vibrations.

"Doesn't the idea of California make you want to vomit?" Mark asked. He'd lost so much weight, his eyes bulged and the black kohl around them effected a mask, and he looked, she thought, handsome, sort of like a panda bear. The love of a good boy had changed him, he said. In his photographs now the transvestites and bar people looked at the camera and smiled. Almost Mona Lisas. Mark still frequented the pissoirs—he and his boyfriend had an agreement—and he still liked it rough, but not with his one and only. Their apartment was filled with toys and old pictures and ornate lamps. Mark had blown up bits of Sontag's essay and used it to paper the wall over the couch. "The camp eye has the power to transform experience." "It's not all in the eye of the beholder." "It is the farthest extension in sensibility of the metaphor of life as theater." He told her that what he had read to her before in the bar might be the beginning of a play he was writing. "There's a part for you. If you're willing." "Oh, you know I'm willful," she answered.

Ruth finished her letter to Grace, which had taken nearly two weeks of her time. Not every minute, of course. It just sat on the kitchen table, pushed to the side, brought to the center, and pushed aside again, for all that time. She never asks about her brother who's in Vietnam fighting for her. He'd even volunteered. Ruth was proud of him. What had Grace said when she was told. She said he was an idiot. She wouldn't care if he lived or died. Or me, for that matter. She's mean and wild. Ruth's letter spoke none of this, just a few cautionary words and a certain tone about the news about her brother. What was the point in fighting anymore.

Mark insisted she wouldn't have to memorize anything. All she would have to do was read the lines. Maybe wear a costume. Her hospital uniform. She was to be the good nurse who ministered to his soul, but who was also the bad nurse after dark. She could change wigs, or something. Acting was a kind of lying and telling the truth at the same time. Whenever Grace lied, she did it so well, she believed it. Maybe that's why Bill's letter hadn't bothered her. She believed everything she had said to him and forgot it just as fast. Lying was a way to get out of the house, away from the fights, and it came so naturally, it didn't feel like lying. So if lies weren't lies, what was the truth. It was all right Mark saying there wasn't one truth, that's easy to accept, but she was talking about her insides, knowing what she felt from what she didn't feel.

Grace listened to Ellen, who was repeating her own name and her mother's name and a bunch of other words. Today she wasn't talking the way she could if she wanted to. Grace was sure Ellen tried on some days and decided not to try on other days. She could be self-conscious, even critical. But then she'd lapse, disappear. She'd come out of it and return as if she had been away. "Dead," Ellen put it. "*Night of the Living Dead*, except I'm the living and the living dead. They win most of the time. That's why I might as well be dead." Ellen asked her if she thought that being alive was like being dead but inside out. Then she asked, "Do you think it's right to grow flowers? I don't." She yelled and stamped her feet, agitated again. One of Ellen's most spectacular episodes was the time she ripped all the geraniums out of the window boxes on the doctor's homes in the rich part of town. She tore down ivy, too, very methodically getting every vine, and no one did anything but watch. A crowd grew and the doctors' maids and nurses peered out the windows and doors and shook their heads but no one said anything to Ellen or even called the cops. A young black woman pulling out flowers from window boxes and tearing down fifty-year-old ivy, that's a devastating sight, a peek into possession, a particular violence and no one could think of anything to say about it. Not even, What are you doing, because in a way everyone knew what she was doing and why. Ellen told Grace that she stared some of the onlookers down, waiting, daring them. But nothing. She'd been given day privileges but now she wouldn't get them anymore.

Grace wrote Celia that she didn't think of Ellen as female or male. Maybe she didn't think she was human. Sometimes Grace walked through the big arch, away from the hospital, and looked back at the floor where Ellen lived. Looked for her window and imagined her lying on her bed, talking to herself or just silent. She never had sexy thoughts about Ellen but wondered if Ellen did—about anyone. These thoughts she had about women. When she looked at their breasts like a man. Were they her thoughts. She couldn't tell. It was like lying and telling the truth. Where does a thought come from? Where does the sound, the moan of sex, come from? She asked Celia if she did what she wanted to do.

Maybe indiscretion was the better part of valor. Grace wanted to run at her own discretion. She wanted to be loose and to be held. Her fantasies, she confided to Mark, were the usual crap. Me, Jane, you, Tarzan, tie me up, slap me a little, show me that I like it. Be reckless and then be held accountable. Held down, maybe even punished. "That's the way love is," Mark sang.

When Grace got drunk enough she told some guy to follow her, as if she were Lauren Bacall telling Bogey all he had to do was whistle. That's the way love is. "You go through men like a hot knife through butter," Mark went on. "Isn't it the other way around," she laughed, "or can I be the knife?" Sitting at the bar, images running rampant, one abandoning another, she looked at a woman who was looking at a woman who was looking at a man. That's the way love is. So she'd want some guy to follow her, as if they were playing a grown-up game of hide-and-seek, except what's there to discover. The blond at the end of the bar had a small pointed pink tongue and an expression like a schnauzer. Grace hated schnauzers. You set up a chase. Then get trapped. Mark said that sophistication meant an intelligent distance from joy. Or was that jaded. The way that woman was looking at that man. So soft, her guts hanging out. There's a rock & roll dream in your heart. She watched them fit their bodies together. You're Mick Jagger and everybody wants you. You can get anybody. The woman's hand moved down his back. He pressed his knee between her legs. Grace thought about Splendor in the Grass, that moment when Natalie Wood, after getting out of the nuthouse, walks away from Warren Beatty, looks toward her friends waiting in the car, and Warren goes back to his pregnant and barefoot wife, and there's some heat between them, something about animals.

She spoke to the guy next to her. She said he could follow her, later. He turned out to have two fingers missing on his right hand, which he didn't show her until nearly the end of the night, and then, very deliberately, shoved the hand up to her face, saying, "My therapist says I should make a point of…" It made it worse. Grace realized he hadn't used that hand at all. He'd kept it in his lap, drinking with the same hand that he'd touched her with. Just as they're about to go, he brings it out and waves it in her face. It was like a trick. Or entrapment. I wouldn't have cared, she told Mark, if he hadn't hidden it. Everybody's got something to hide.

Chapter 8

Jane writes: I want to remember in order to keep from being an animal. I'm sure animals have hardly any memory except for those exceptional ones that find their way home, travel hundreds of miles and return after months. If I forget things and sensations, and memories become less exact, I'll be an animal, like everyone else. It wasn't that Jane didn't like animals. Domestic animals meant a kind of servitude she couldn't stand. Dogs on leashes, having to be walked, a dog's life.

Jimmy writes: Call me Ishmael. Call me Tom Sawyer. Call me Adam. Call me Roy Rogers. Call me Tarzan. Call me Dick Tracy. Call me Dick.

Jimmy dressed slowly. He had nowhere to go, except to his theater, which was like going nowhere. These mornings he awoke with his hand on his cock, cradling it like a baby. Sometimes it'd be stiff—and sometimes he'd take care of it, like it was his baby, sometimes he'd ignore it, as if it were a pest. It depended on his mood, which today was shabby, like his room, with its few really good antiques saved from the store, with the pictures of Marlene Dietrich over the bed, the ones from *The Devil Is a Woman*. He'd seen Jane last night and it was as it usually was. They saw two double features and after that it was late or early and he couldn't take it, her, the situation, anywhere and she couldn't either. But she acted as if there was nowhere for the situation to go. He said again, You do want to make love with me. And she got out of it as she always did. He didn't know what he wanted either. Somehow here was this girl he'd known since they were kids, and she was still around. She was convinced their relationship meant something. Not that she'd say something as direct as that. His last year in high school, he'd called her, because he was miserable and she asked him something which he refused to answer, and she got so upset at his silence that he went over to see her and they went for a long drive and he talked more than he ever had to her but that was the last time really that that had happened. He had opened up. Opened up, Jimmy thought, like my antique store, then it closed up, now the cinema…

He finally put his pants on, looking at himself in the mirror. He looked better, he thought, than he felt. Except for his teeth which he knew were dead giveaways. Jane was more interested in the past than he was. It was kind of a personal treasure to her, her past, and he was included in that. He had his jacket on. He looked at himself again. I suppose I look like a man, he thought, and walked out the door.

Jane lingered on the past, entirely disinterested in something called the future. It had absolutely no meaning to her. Jimmy and his science fiction, his teasing her about walking, no, running, backward in time. Jane telling him that there was just as much invention in versions of the past as in what's written about the future.

Uncle Larry explained again that their mother kicked their father out of the house, which was why, he went on, he slept in his mother's bed until he was thirteen. "I was the baby of the family, like you, kid," he said. Larry was sitting opposite her in the Stage Delicatessen, a favorite hangout of his. They ate like demons. Larry was telling her the story of the con men in the forties, during the war, when everyone was out to make a buck. "This guy came to see your father and me, you see, and he said, 'All these American soldiers have died and there's a warehouse full of coats, jackets, that can be bought for a penny.' So your father and I went to meet him in Chicago but he wanted a lot of money right then, up front, you know, and we had to think about it, we said, and he couldn't wait. So we didn't lose our shirts on that one." "Tell me the Scottsdale story again." Larry lit his cigar and breathed expansively, his big stomach coming up, like the sun, out of his pants. "Yeah, well, for a while I thought I might like to be a cowboy—you see me and your father as cowboys?—and I was going to a ranch out there, in Arizona. Now, nothing was happening out there back then, nothing. And they offered to sell me the ranch and a lot of land for a song. But your father couldn't see leaving New York and living on the land. It would have been like, I don't know, like…" "Like going back to Russia?" Jane asked. "Yeah, leaving the city… Anyway, if we'd have bought that ranch, we'd be sitting pretty. Zsa Zsa Gabor's got a jewelry shop out there, it's a watering hole for the rich. But you've heard this story a million times, Jane. I feel like I'm telling you a fairy tale." Jane's pants felt uncomfortably tight. "I guess it is like a fairy tale to me, about the past."

Larry popped another Dexamyl and paid the check. Jane asked him if she seemed like a real girl to him. Larry laughed and reminded her that she didn't have to do anything to be a girl. She was born that way. Jane continued, "But haven't you ever wondered if you were a boy or a man?" Larry puffed harder and took a fast right to beat the light. "One time," she told him, "'I was sitting with a couple of guys and they said, about the waitress, she's a real girl." "Are you still a virgin?" he asked. Jane looked out the window and said yes. "Maybe when you're not a virgin you'll feel more like a girl or a woman," Larry answered. "Can I be more of a girl?" she asked. "It's supposed to be easier in Samoa," Larry went on. "I'm not even sure what you're asking." He pulled into a space in front of her apartment. Jane bent over to kiss her uncle's big face, bigger than her father's, and not as handsome. "You're my kind of girl, how's that, sweetheart?" His face was as full as the moon.

I remember, wrote Jane, that summer when I was eight. There was a twelve-year-old boy, very cute, dark hair. He'd just become tall and had stretch marks on his back, right at his waist. I liked his friend better than him; his friend was blond, like Troy Donahue. Or Tab Hunter. The dark-haired one was always with the blond one, around the pool. One day the blond wasn't around and the dark one came over to me. We went for a walk on the beach. When no one was around he threw me down on the sand and sat on my stomach. He said, Kiss me. I kissed him. He said, No, like this. And he stuck his tongue in my mouth. Then a woman walked by and he threw sand in my face. We were just supposed to be playing. Child's play. He told me that I looked like his sister. I immediately thought that that was a strange, a queer thing to say, and decided that there was something wrong with him. Something was wrong with him. I didn't tell anyone that I'd had my first adult kiss, but I knew that's what it was.

The mirror Sinuway had given her cracked when Jimmy sat on it. Jane looked into it anyway. Jimmy said she was a reliquary at nineteen. A person, she told him, cannot be a reliquary. He told her in his terms a person could. He didn't care about the definition. "People," he said, "fill themselves up, with memories, with things." "You mean the mind is a reliquary." "Some minds," he said. "Are you saying that

99

remembering things keeps you from thinking new thoughts?" "I guess so," he said. "I don't think the mind is like that," Jane said. "And you," he said, "probably believe that a person can love in unlimited amounts." "I don't know," she said, "I never thought about that."

People fill in the gaps left by other people, who you loved and who disappeared. Jane had lost friends—, she thought, as if I mislaid them. Now that his girlfriend was in New York, she saw less of Felix. But he wasn't gone. Not lost, at least not yet. His eyes were a cracked blue-grey. She assumed that was from acid. Her mind wandered as her teacher spoke. Old Testament class led by a woman who appeared to have leaped out of that part of the Bible. The idea that the Bible was a written thing, a thing of men, was hard to imagine. What was the impulse they'd felt—, J, and the other letters who stood for the men—how had it been carried from one author to another? What were the circumstances? Now the teacher was describing a war and every time she said bloody she laughed and all the students laughed back and she laughed some more. She's very nervous, Jane thought, Professor Rathmere, an ancient herself, a scholar of the old school, a spinster, a noble spinster. Her life was as incomprehensible to Jane as those of the authors of the Bible. Not as incomprehensible, but relatively so. Relatively. Rathmere was still smiling and laughing and describing battles. Her uncle had slept in the same bed with his mother until he was thirteen.

The devil is a television set at the end of the bed. She's still a virgin, Jimmy reminded himself, and he didn't want the responsibility. I don't lust for her. Or anyone. Diana was the patroness of hunting and virginity, an odd combination. She protected the hunter and hunted. Jimmy didn't think of himself as a hunter, but he thought Jane thought of herself as hunted. Maybe she didn't. Maybe he thought of her as hunted, virgins being the only prey left.

What makes him think he can have a new idea, Jane wondered. Her clothes were on the couch and her books on the floor. She was moving uptown, out of her sister's apartment to a house in Riverdale rented by a group of people, only one of whom she knew. Jimmy thought she was crazy to move so far away, but she had to get out fast, that's what her sister said. The house in Riverdale faced the Hudson, and was so big, one could feel alone. Jane felt eccentric in her room that had a window seat. It provoked her to have antiquated ideas, Gothic ideas. Jimmy as her perverted suitor, her Heathcliff, morbid, brooding. She wanted to divest herself of her virginity so that she could give herself to him. But first she had to find a man to fuck.

People make too much of sex, Larry had said. To Jane it felt like something that had to be overcome, or at least gotten over, like a headache or a toothache. She had been attracted to a thin, tall guy with sort of bad teeth like Jimmy's and had spoken to him at a party. An hour passed and they were still talking. A slightly older man wearing a fat tie with a Greek column down its center took her hand and drew her to the side of the room. "I'm jealous," he said. "Jealous?" "Yes," he said, "I brought him." Her body moved backward, toward the wall, as if to indicate that she didn't mean to stand in his way. "I didn't know." And she didn't.

Most of the people in the house at Riverdale were research psychologists or classical musicians. Jane was the only college girl. To get rid of my virginity, I have to lose weight, she thought, but found it impossible in the house, where, with so many people around, someone was always eating. One of the research psychologists was a thin man with thick glasses. He had the cleanest room. Whenever Jane passed his door she looked in. The bed was always made and nothing was out of order. The books were stacked in even piles. The pens were in a holder. What distressed her most was that his shoes were always exactly in the same place under his chair, equidistant from the legs of the chair, and lined up precisely with the back of the chair. He never said too much but, like his room, whatever he said was in order. They all had dinners together, and Jane became friends with Ollie, a violinist with flat feet. At night when she couldn't sleep he'd come to her gothic bedchamber and play, at her request, her favorite lullabye: Rockabye and good night with roses and lilies. Her grandmother's name was Rose, and her aunt's name was Lillie, and slowly she'd fall asleep while Ollie fiddled in the doorway. Jimmy's mother requested an appointment with him, and they met at a decent bar, her words for his choice, at the base of the Empire State Building, Jimmy remembering that Jane had told him she used to meet her sisters at the base of the building and never having looked up, didn't know that the tallest building in the world rose above her. What a dope, he thought, as his mother ordered a whiskey sour and asked about the cinema. It's going all right, he answered. Crow's feet on her, looked to him like the footprints of a small bird pressed onto thin skin. She was thin-skinned. After her second whiskey sour she complained about his father, and placed her pale hand on his, a dirty male version of hers. He felt like a male version of her in all respects, and always agreed with her assessments of his father. In complicity he drank down another beer. Her lipstick had smeared slightly and her speech slurred and he thought she was the most beautiful woman he'd ever seen. When he left her in Penn Station at Track 19 he felt he could see through her, read her thoughts, and he turned abruptly, went to a phone booth and called Maurice, who said he was free for dinner and did Jimmy want some too?

Her father reading Lord Chesterfield to her, at bedtime, like Polonius to Ophelia, giving advice in order to repress her, this was not an easy thing to explain to Uncle Larry, who said, "When your father was very little, he always protected me. I was his baby brother. But he wasn't that big himself. We were only fifteen months apart. And we lived in a rough neighborhood. You don't know anything about that, they protected you from that." Larry had lost at the races again. "Our mother never combed her hair, that's why when he sees yours, he goes a little nuts." Larry paused and puffed. "You do comb it when you see him, don't you?" "When I see him, I comb it, Larry." The men in the family didn't lose their hair; it was a source of pride to them. They kept their hair and lost at the races and lost in business. "The textile industry," Larry was going on, "used to be lots of smalltime people. Till the mid-fifties. Then the big guys moved in—or was it horizontal, monopolies—bought everything—mills, the cotton, the department stores, everything. There wasn't any place for the little guy. And your father didn't want to sell. And by the time he wanted to sell, it was too late. The story of my life, sweetheart."

Jimmy was acting like a real jerk. Saying he'd meet her, then not showing up, or showing up much later. His excuse was that he didn't like her castle on the Hudson. She didn't think it was that. She thought he was angry at her. What was it he said? She was reading things into it. She put down her diary and stared straight ahead. The phone started ringing and she ran to answer it.

The research psychologist with the cleanest room had driven into a concrete wall; it appeared to have been deliberate, onlookers said, said the cop. Onlookers wasn't a word you heard much outside this kind of dialogue and Jane found herself fixing on it. She had looked in on him. "Jimmy thinks I read too much into things," she told Felix when they met accidentally on a street corner in the East Village. His eyes looked even more cracked and his bones were sticking up, almost saluting from his face. "You've got a weird imagination," he told her, "but you're still a virgin, and that's shit, and you still think that Jimmy is a valentine, when he's more full of shit than you are." "I'm not a virgin," she lied. "Okay, let's go to my place." "What about your girlfriend?" Felix told her that was his problem, not hers. Jane looked carefully into those cracked eyes. She hadn't seen him in a while. Felix played with the buttons of her pea jacket and whispered that the best way it could happen would be with him. "In France," he said, "an older man, a friend of the family, usually does it." A horse being broken struggled on the sidewalk before Jane's eyes and she declared, adamantly, "I'm not attracted to you." Felix refused to believe her, his ego at that moment as big as the Alps were high. He relented. "Then let's get a cup of coffee and go to a movie." Jane placed her hand in his—he said, "Your hands are very small"—inside her she knew that there was no way in hell that Felix would ever be considered a friend in her family.

Chapter 9

Emily was in her room, lying on the bed and reading further into the mind of John Winthrop. Did he love his wife too much? How could one be good and show it, make it visible, apart from accumulating a fortune? The good are famous because they're known, but are the famous good, and is that why, once they're famous, they're examined so carefully, so critically? America as the visible kingdom of the righteous. "All labored hard and some by so doing amassed great wealth or won fame among their fellow men—never dared enjoy it... Puritanism required that man refrain from sin but told him he would sin anyhow ... The evil of the world was incurable and inevitable... Winthrop's life vibrated dizzily between indulgence and restraint." Emily wrote these lines from Morgan's book, *The Puritan Dilemma*, in her notebook, where she kept ideas that she would use later, in papers or poems. She wondered if people ever footnoted quotes in poems or just made references that everyone was supposed to know or look up. Writing a poem was supposed to be different from writing a paper. Indulgence and restraint were not, it seemed to Emily, the parameters of her life. That evil might be incarnate, that we might sin even if under restraint, that it might all be incurable, left her in a hollow mood, some of which she expressed to Edith as they watched *Our Town* on television. Emily felt sorry for John Winthrop, his struggle between good and evil, her duel carried with a different fervor.

First of all, what was good and what was bad? Just think of all the witches they burned, Edith dutifully reminded her tenant, who she thought needed to toughen up at the edges. Hadn't that English musician told Emily that anyone could see the red crosses in her blue eyes, and though she bought dark glasses, she would never be able to disguise them.

Edith and Emily finished another box of Royal Lunch crackers. Not salty, Edith noted to herself, looking at her stomach, while Emily glanced in the direction of her own and wondered if she might be pregnant. That English musician, and now they didn't even sleep together anymore, which was a certain kind of irony that would be anathema to John Winthrop, whom she knew would have no sympathy for her. What would she do about it if it were true. She didn't mention this to Edith, whose eyes had filled like swimming pools as she cried silently. Edith was of course thinking about her husband and Emily made a mental note that *Our Town* was a kind of pornography, playing so graphically on morbidity and sentiment. Emily conjured up Nora, who had not died but whom she not saw again sitting under the kitchen table, her hand to her heart, waiting for her heart to stop.

Death had never touched Emily, except if she were to count the time she heard that mother scream upon finding her three-year-old-daughter dead in bed. From walking pneumonia, her own mother told her, saying, again, there's nothing to fear but fear itself and tucking her into bed, as if to keep her from falling into the arms of God or the devil, whoever it is that takes little children away. But death, she recognized, had not really touched her. Edith's eyes were dry and she was tired. So was Emily, whose thoughts kept her awake for several more hours.

Starting to read just before going out or starting a poem with her coat on, Emily found it hard to tell what was intended and what was not. In her own utterances. In Christine's. For some years she held an idea in her mind—could jump high and for long distances, if she let herself. For instance, she could, if she wanted, fly down subway stairs. She held the idea very far away as she might put it; it was never enunciated. Then it occurred to her that it was a fantasy or a dream, existing just below the surface of what was real. But what was real.

Her history professor looked at her and said, "What are you thinking about? The Constitution?" I can't stay suspended in the air was the answer. But she said, "There's no way that the Constitution could be interpreted strictly nearly two hundred years after it was written and it doesn't matter what the Founding Fathers intended. Circumstances change." Back to intention. American history was a refuge from the present, a distant impersonal past that occasionally spills into the present making her absorption in it reasonable, justifiable. She argued about the American Revolution as if it were going on. And much of the time Emily felt herself to be a suitor to ideas, to Christine, to her infrequent boyfriends, even to Edith.

The man Edith had slept with was the childless author of books on children. He didn't, Edith silently agreed with her tenant, particularly like children, but that appealed to Edith, whose own children had given her enough trouble to warrant her some complicity with him. He was an educator, not a father, something she'd pointed out to Emily, who thought it was weird that he wrote about kids when he didn't have them. Her education had not prepared her for millions of things, like living after the dead. She threw her head back, sharply, grabbed her tennis racket, and headed for the park. It was a great day to be alive, sort of.

The thirty or more years between Emily and Edith turned particular discussions into dead ends. Why Emily allowed that rock & roll musician to live on her floor some of the time was beyond Edith. After two weeks they had stopped having sex, which Edith didn't know (and never would have dreamed); they had had it, and then it was over, and Emily got her period. Weighing it in her mind: first, there was sex, then there wasn't; nothing reached an agreeable balance, as if the facts of a relationship could be weighed like a bunch of bananas. He'd bought her dinner and now he didn't buy her dinner. He had had compunctions about doing sexual things with her she had barely any feelings about, had never considered. It's when you get told things over and over that you hold opinions about them. Emily wrote: If you have principles, you don't have to think. She looked forward to his almost comforting biweekly nocturnal visits, during which she and he behaved like priest and nun, and Emily fantasized them into the literature about the hue and false. Fidessa, Duessa. The red crosses in her eyes had nothing to do, in his mind, with the Red Cross Knight, but she made that reference. He was not a knight in shining armor, although his dark eyes did shine and look wet sometimes; she told herself she wasn't looking for one anyway.

Christine didn't like the musician much, but then Emily didn't like Christine's boyfriend, either, and it appeared that best friends often didn't like each other's boyfriends, though why was part of a mystery Emily supposed would one day be revealed. She had faith that, as she grew up, life's intricacies would unravel like a skein of wool in front of more sophisticated eyes. She assumed she was not ready for many things which was why she didn't feel exactly what she thought she should. And then she had feelings for which she had no reasons, feelings that no one had spoken to her about. She thought her relationship with Christine, for instance, might be unusual.

The musician was cryptic, with little education or interest in anything other than music, which he squandered, his teachers cried, on the likes of rock & roll. Movies on Forty- second Street at 1 A.M. gave a semblance of adventure to what Emily thought was a too normal, too ordered existence. The English musician's group came out with a record and he was more insecure than ever. Emily was nurse to his wounds, imagined or real. The record producer punched their singer in the booth. He was exhausted, that's why he was yellow, not because he had hepatitis again. His life was a diversion from her own, which was piled with books and unwritten poems and not-yet-handed-in papers. He, she supposed, lived in the present, but she preferred to live just a little behind the times, while being present at what was new, like a guest at an elaborately produced meal. Christine disagreed, urging Emily to get out of her house, not just to see him at 1 A.M., not just to see a movie. No one had ever cared so much about her as Christine did, Emily decided, and she was always in her mind, a reference point for her days, home base for her nights.

Opposites attract, not just between the sexes but within them, Emily determined, supporting her face in her hands. It didn't really bother her that Christine didn't like him. Emily was not mad with love. Dispassionately she rode the subway to the Cloisters and with her took *Mansfield Park* and the long subway ride was an empty, endless room filled with people who argued about whether or not acting was a corrupting influence, particularly on young women, because lines that were not true were spoken from their lips. They dissembled. When Emily applied cream to her face and hands she studied her skin, which didn't yet have any lines. She wanted to have great, deep lines when she was old but she hoped her cheekbones would hold the skin up, much as a clothesline holds up clothes. When I have lines they'll be my part, like an actor's part. The English musician had compared her with Edith Sitwell, whose eccentricity was one day to be matched by Emily's, he teased. Emily considered that a compliment, even though she felt he could never understand how she was different, but nevertheless, she monologued in front of the Unicorn Tapestry, nevertheless, being eccentric is taking liberties. And give me liberty or give me death.

Emily's favorite history teacher might have appreciated Emily's spouting that tired line in a medieval setting. Professor Wilson had announced on her first day teaching the freshmen that she didn't want to be their friend, just their teacher, and Emily decided to become her friend. She set about on this quest and announced it to Christine, who insisted that Emily shouldn't expect everyone to love her. Emily demurred, rebelling passively against the suggestion, hearing someone else inside her chant, Love is only a word and beauty is only a word and sticks and stones may break my bones, but words will never hurt me. That was a lie. More than anything else words hurt. That's why I really hate words, and then aloud told Christine that she had written a line, "Wordlessly we stalk words," and after this conversation would develop it. Christine, studying psychology and philosophy, talked about Jung. Had he really been a Nazi? He had written "No matter how much the parents, etc., have sinned against the child, the adult who is really adult will accept these sins as his own condition which has to be reckoned with. Only a fool is interested in other people's guilt, since he cannot alter it. The wise learn only from their own guilt." Each thought about the other and their friendship, which elicited dark thoughts and feelings, as well as the opposite.

The other's position was somehow more advantageous. Emily was an only child, envied by Christine, who had a younger brother, who was envied by Emily, who felt deprived of a real family. One had money, the other didn't. One had a living father, the other didn't. Together they dissected the minutiae of their lives, often stressing their similarities or muting their differences to make them seem more like likenesses. People called each by the other's name, even though they didn't look alike, and Christine more than Emily found it disturbing. It was as if, in Christine's eyes, Emily was doing something to make that happen. On the other hand, Christine was more successful with men, and when they were out together Emily found herself receding to the back of the booth. She's more beautiful than I am, Emily concluded sadly, and was angry at Christine involuntarily. But men were supposed to occupy a separate, defined space that did not intrude upon their friendship. The day turned into evening and the evening, night, and the best friends talked and talked. Why, Emily wondered, had love taken the form it did. Why had dying for love become one of the conventions. And was it really necessary to suffer a broken heart. When had we learned to. Even suffering, crying, sounds different in different countries and we react to pain with different sounds when we speak different languages.

Edith watched their relationship like a mother cat who is no longer feeding her kittens. She knew trouble when she saw it, but there was no way, hardly even the words with which to broach the subject with Emily, who was more sensitive than she had ever been. Allowed to be more sensitive. For certainly if Edith had grown up in a household where there had been more money, she might have been gentler, she thought. In a way that Edith couldn't fathom, Emily could sense her, knew when to avoid her, or knew how to talk with her when she didn't want anyone near her. The quality was remarkable, but there was no future in being sensitive, no future in poetry, or even in prophecy. But children—and Emily was still a child—didn't think about the future and money, especially Emily, whose father, a lawyer, kept her allowance coming despite any problems he or her mother might have about the way Emily dressed or the people she saw. Probably Ethical Culture—she said he was a Quaker—Edith thought as she stacked the toilet paper in the utility closet, which took up half the shelf space, but such a bargain and now she wouldn't have to think about toilet paper for half a year at least. Unless she threw a lot of dinner parties, but she didn't imagine she would.

The sun came through Emily's bathroom window and cast light on her face and his. He was sleeping on the floor, on a thin sheet of foam rubber he called his pallet, his bed when he was with her. His guitar was under her bed. When she opened her eyes she saw his black underpants. Bikinis. He slept with his back toward her, his long body below her like a rug of flesh. She'd missed another sixteenth-century poetry class. She grabbed her robe to cover herself. He walked around naked in front of her. Christine said he was a tease. But she hated him anyway. His body. She told herself she didn't care. Love isn't like this. She kicked him in the ass. If your people hadn't left England we might not all want to be famous.

The child educator called on Edith just often enough to satisfy something, but she would never again consider marriage. She admitted to herself that she was comfortable with her life, not content; there were longings. But she liked waking up and going out and answering to no one. There was a way in which feeling loss kept her husband with her, and she didn't want to give him up. Loss had a shape, a presence she didn't have to share with anyone. When you get older you don't want to have to share with anyone. She could be as selfish as she wanted. She walked around the apartment, turning off the lights. All those anymores. Could she raise Emily's rent two dollars a week to keep up with the electric bills? It's still a good idea. Edith ran her fingers through her short thick hair. It had never curled when she was a child and now she wore it as she liked it, close to her head, the shape of which she was proud. Her hair was convenient. Like having a woman in to clean the apartment once a week, something she hadn't done when her husband was alive. Hiring the black woman caused her conflict. Hadn't she marched for civil rights as early as the forties. Shouldn't she hire a white woman, but the state employment agency sent her Helen, who was about her age, and Helen needed the work. And why should Edith stand on principle when to do so meant denying this woman a source of income, and by now they'd been together, she and Helen, six years, and how could she have fixed the world by not hiring her. Edith sighed audibly in the empty apartment and left a note for Helen—son had been sick, maybe heroin, but Edith didn't ask—and ran her hands once more through her hair. A trace of lipstick still on her lips, she added some more orange and smiled at herself, as if pleased not with her image but with something else that was not pictured.

Helen and Emily met in the kitchen and had some coffee that Edith had left for Helen. Or maybe it was just left over. Helen asked Emily how her poems and painting were going and Emily asked Helen about her son. Emily wondered if Helen really liked Edith, if she could really like her. Not wanting Helen to see Keith lying on the floor, she walked backward into the room, blocking the door as she talked, almost stepping on his head. Helen wanted one of Emily's paintings and Emily was touched. Helen laughed about it later, Emily walking backward, hiding her guy. White people were so funny. Her son got angry when she said funny. When Helen brought home the painting she'd asked Emily for, to go over the couch, her son walked out of the apartment.

Or so Emily imagined it. Gazing into a mirror, absentmindedly plucking her eyebrows, the disorder on her brow, Emily removed as much of the present as she could. The piano teacher is sitting beside her now on the soft chair she liked so much, her clothes like a garden that needs tending. Full of color and the smell of violets, Hilda's mouth is slightly open and she is smiling as Emily plays, not too badly, a Bach exercise. As Emily finishes the piece without a mistake, Hilda is almost triumphant. No mistakes. The forest across the street appears, seen again as it was during every lesson. With longing. Her own eyebrows and Hilda's clothes now resonant of Richard II with those gardening metaphors for bad governing. No mistakes. We can't make any mistakes. How can I avoid them? Her eyes close and Hilda fades reluctantly and again she wonders where she is right now and.

Part IV

Chapter 10

Remember walking on the sidewalk and jumping over the cracks, and if you lose your balance, if you step on one, something terrible will happen to you. Walking a fine line invisible to anyone but herself, Jane dropped out of college and got a job at Macy's, in the toy department, where she expected never to see anyone she knew. She was living with her sister again, eating whole wheat donuts for lunch and finishing boxes of chocolate cookies for dinner. Home was a room that was too empty. The chair was uncomfortable. The air smelled bad, like a new apartment, although it wasn't. The shower didn't have enough pressure. Next door an alcoholic couple screamed into the night. Jane watched television and wrote in her diary.

If I loved somebody I wouldn't feel like this. Or if somebody loved me. Sometimes I feel there's no difference between my body and this chair I'm sitting in. In a funny way I don't think I exist. Not really. Things just seem to go on and on, with and without me, mostly without me.

Her father's family, Larry insisted, was full of lively, dramatic people. Melodramatic maybe. The facts about her father's family were, Jane supposed, not unusual. They arrived in this country and couldn't speak the language. The oldest brother, born in Russia, escaped on foot, crossing a river on his uncle's back. The two younger brothers—are a family of sons—and Marty, her father, were born in America. The family had escaped so that the men wouldn't have to fight in the Czar's army. There are then three sons, a flamboyant, perhaps mad mother and a benign father who doesn't live with them. Kicked out. Or lives with them sometimes. He visits once a week. They cohabit, Larry puts it, once a week. Still, the mother advertises for a husband in the Yiddish newspapers, which none of the sons can read. They are not taught the language, nor are they bar mitzvahed. It's early in the twentieth century and they want to be Americans. No one knows what an American is and across the Atlantic Gertrude Stein is working on that very problem. But they wouldn't know this.

From her view behind the Barbie doll counter Christmas was a TV series of family conflicts. A little girl points her finger at a Barbie doll outfit and her mother points to another. "Don't you want this one?" The little girl looks at the other one. She starts to want both. She can't make up her mind. Her mother gets angry. "Just choose one. You can't have them both." Close up on the child's face, just about to cry. They buy the one the mother wanted.

The floor supervisor, a young dark-haired man, wears a white boutonniere as all the supervisors do. Some of the salespeople have worked at Macy's ten (red flower) or twenty (white flower) years. The saleswomen remind Jane of sturdy ships that sail into and out of harbor, the fifth floor, resignation their port of call. Resignation keeps her alert to resignation. Frank, the floor supervisor, flirts with her, giving her knowing, we-shouldn't-be-working-here looks to which she responds coyly. She decides he's the one. He will be the man, not Jimmy. She knows him too well, and anyway, he's just a child. He's also too skinny.

Grandma Rose wears her hair piled on top of her head. It's a big mess, always falling down, the combs slipping out. She's constantly raising her hands to her head to push them back in and it's always futile. She married her husband in Russia quickly, after the son of the lord who owned the land they worked took a liking to her and wanted to kiss her hand. She gave him her hand but wouldn't take off her glove because he was a Christian. She was supposed to have been beautiful. Jane tried to imagine her grandmother, who later covered newspapers with towels and bits of cloth to keep the people in the pictures warm, extending a gloved hand to the lord's son. The two images could be placed side by side, but could not be superimposed to make a whole, and looking from one to the other was like reading two different languages in the same sentence when you don't know one of them. When she arrived in America, New York, she was a young woman with a husband and child. They lived on the Lower East Side. Larry and Marty are born on Ludlow Street.

Sam Wo's is not far from the Lower East Side. As usual it's crowded and as usual Felix was pricking certain ideas that he had said littered the landscape. In his way he was much more romantic than Jane, but not about love, about life, which he wanted to experience madly. Madness bored Jane. She didn't think that mad people were so great or so beautiful. Felix could talk to her about Artaud until he himself got locked up, she would resist these insights. My grandmother was mad, she told him, but you wouldn't have wanted to spend time with her. Felix wouldn't tell Jane anything about his family because his father was a famous artist and he thought that would make a difference. "Why should it make a difference to me?" she insisted. "I don't want to be an artist." "It might make a difference to

Jimmy," Felix said. Maybe Jimmy, she considered, he takes his heroes so seriously.

Everything Jimmy read conspired to equip him with outrageous notions about men, himself. Kerouac cut into the heroic grand figure but created another type, the one Jimmy aspired to. Then there was Bob Dylan. If he'd been born in the Midwest, and not Long Island, Jimmy might have had a chance to be either one of those guys. As a European, Felix argued against the tyranny of influence, of tradition, while Jimmy, an American, perceived nothing except for what he chose as influence. And Jane sat between them, stationed in the balance, drinking coffee in Ukrainian restaurants. Their arguments were often about the ineffable and she found herself speechless in the face of Felix's libertarian absoluteness and Jimmy's veiled masculine strivings. It was enough to be aware and that, like the Salk vaccine, would protect one from false hope, from bullshit. Jane listened as if from very far away. It seemed to have nothing to do with her.

She tried to visualize her father when he was a little boy. Hazel-eyed, with thick black hair, small for his age, he's sent by his mother to find coal in the dark basement that may have rats in it. He's terrified of rats and the dark basement. Being sent there by his mother was terrible, a descent into a children's hell, the hellish imagination that grows wild when not tended. He was his mother's favorite, Larry says, and very guilty about it. Is fear catching? Is guilt? Jane wanted to understand the patterns as eccentricities or commonplaces, to understand the ties between siblings and parents, between siblings and each other. She and her sisters, her father and his brothers. Her mother rarely talks about her family except to say that her own mother was perfect. The children of that mother don't seem to like each other nearly as much as Larry and Marty do, their tie is remarkable, unending, intangible, in the blood, Larry says.

Right after Jimmy woke up, when his face hadn't set yet, and he'd been up all night on speed, he thought he saw a trace of Bob Dylan. Ouspensky said a man could go mad looking at a broken ashtray, or was it a dirty ashtray, or could it be your own mirror when you look into it to see the person you wish you were. I want to be famous and she wants to be thin. What about the image reflected back at you, yourself in someone else's mirror, a reflection you don't recognize. Jane talked about not recognizing herself and together they took hundreds of pictures in photo booths. Jimmy had a few on his mirror. Jane posed in profile, certain that one side off her face was thinner, while Jimmy would drop his down, and look up only with his eyes, a cigarette hanging from his lips, a la Belmondo. He couldn't understand why she was so attached to her family and bothered to remember or to write down the facts as she knew them, as she put it. He told her that and she said, It's my family and you don't have to understand.

One afternoon at Macy's Jane was visited by a woman she'd barely even heard of, the wife of the Austrian friend of her sister, the one who had thought of her as a Lolita that summer when she was twelve. The visit was unannounced. The woman was small, like the man, and she and Jane drank coffee in the employee cafeteria, sitting at the counter. Jane was on her break. Like her husband, the wife was supposed to be a genius. One of the reasons for their marriage was to produce more geniuses. "We are Skinnerians," she explained to Jane. "But we don't work with rats anymore." The woman looked into Jane's face, studying it as if it were a maze. She asked if Jane liked her husband. She said with pride that her husband wanted her to meet and like the women he was interested in. "He's interested in me?" Jane asked. "Because I don't think of him that way. He's nice, but I've never been attracted to him." Jane announced her answers the way the woman asked the questions, objectively, disinterestedly. The woman paid both checks and said it was good to meet her, hurrying off to her next case, perhaps. Jane didn't test well anyway.

To Jane it was all very European, if disturbing, like art films, like *Rocco and His Brothers* and *8 1/2*. Her sister would be furious. Returning to her position behind the Barbie doll counter, she observed Frank as she sold and didn't sell dolls. She watched him and he watched her. Jane stayed late to find herself alone with him. And once alone, in his office, as he wheeled toward her on the office chair, the recognition of what she was doing shocked her into abeyance, her heart alone giving her life, beating so loudly the room itself seemed alive. The walls were her flesh and she fled.

Jane's parents were introduced by a boy they nicknamed Stiff Jesus, because, her mother explained, he was very skinny and very tall. To this day Marty can remember what Sylvia was wearing when they first met. She has long brown hair, almost to her waist; she plays tennis, rides horses, wants to write and draw. She was always happy, he tells his daughters. Both are in night school, working during the day, trying to get a college education at night. Her father studies Latin and remembers his conjugations. Sylvia works as a secretary. They date for seven years and each time Marty tells his mother, Rose, that they want to get married, Rose drops to the ground and says she's dying. They eat in Chinese restaurants every Sunday and when they fight Marty leaves Sylvia standing in the middle of the street. "After one fight," Larry tells her, "they stopped seeing each other for a whole year and your father cried in his pillow every night." They make up. They neck in the park and are virgins when they marry. Grandma Rose does not drop dead.

I'm gaining weight, Jimmy noticed, getting up in the middle of the day, in the middle of the week. He'd fought with Maurice and Felix, and Jane was working behind a doll counter in a department store. Sometimes she scared him to death. He couldn't figure out what she wanted. Last night he'd called her and she said she'd been reading but it sounded to him as though she were visiting one of her fabled relatives in Russia. He couldn't talk to her. He wished he could just phone up Kerouac and talk to him, but he was rumored to be somewhere in Florida with his wife or mother, watching television and drinking beer, or that's what people said. Sentences flowed out of him, he didn't hold back, it just kept coming. Kerouac could write about a guy he'd just met and what it was like, introduce him to the reader, and then it'd be a dream or a party that he was at with Mardou and they'd be drinking and she'd go home pissed off and he'd come home the next day and on and on. It was all the subject of his work and it was his life. But Jimmy hadn't met a Neal Cassady who could have taught him about life and consequently Jimmy felt he wasn't actually living. He shared this unspoken feeling with Jane. If Jane were around today, he'd see a movie with her. She was good for movies. Like the time they went to see *Broken Blossoms*, in its innocence so consoling to both of them, as if there really existed a time before sex. Annoyed that there wasn't a magic feeling between them, Jimmy walked on ahead, and Jane, not knowing that, clicked her heels slightly as they reached the subway. And she thinks she's not unrealistic, he thought while she thought that holding onto her feelings about him was something outside her control, as was having been born into a dramatic, or crazy, family.

Uncle Larry was complaining about his bleeding ulcer and drinking milk along with a corned beef sandwich. "The combination would make anyone sick," he said. When Jane was a child visiting him and her father at their office on Broadway, Larry seemed so casual and offhand, she never would have suspected an ulcer or imagined that anything could bother him. "Down with the bosses," the two bosses ironically shouted to the salesmen who'd been with them for years. "Down with the bosses," she too yelled. Larry bossed from a big office with a large mahogany desk behind which he sat and looked out the picture window over his city, talking expansively, a cigar in his mouth, his bleeding ulcer his own business. The salesmen pointed in the other direction when she wanted to find her father's office. In a room the size of a generous closet Marty was bent over the roll-top desk covered with bills and dirty pipe cleaners. This other boss always yelled at her to keep her room clean. For reasons Jane never understood, though they were raised in that part of America with the biggest concentration of active socialists, though they shouted down the bosses, they had never even gone to lectures or belonged to the Party when everyone else they knew had. "Socialism seemed European to me," Larry said.

Felix, her European, had done a disappearing act. Jimmy didn't look at her the way she thought she wanted, the way men did in movies, not yet. But Frank did. He looked at her like that. With her heart in her mouth, as if suffering from a toothache, she followed Frank home, pretending, when they met on the subway, that she was going to see a movie at the New Yorker. His apartment was much worse than hers. Depressing, she thought, distracting herself from his overwhelmingly physical presence, even though he was short, for a man, not more than four inches taller than she. Her stockings pulled tight around her thighs. Frank offered her red wine that his family in Buffalo made specially. That's where he was from—ran an Italian restaurant. Big family. Italians in Buffalo. Hadn't she heard about…

She wasn't listening, she was looking everywhere. Into the bottom of her glass, full of red wine that ate into her stomach. Larry told her no one in the family could drink. Frank had reproductions on the wall of flowers painted by Van Gogh, those crazy ones that are in no way pleasant, that are in fact grotesque, though Frank thought they were nice. Jimmy would have laughed at her, noticing these class differences as a way to comfort herself about what she couldn't feel comfortable with: sex. Frank walked toward her and put his hand on her knee. She wondered if he could tell how heavy she was from the way her knee folded over and had flesh on either side. But Frank probably wasn't thinking too long about that because his mouth was on hers and she felt the raw wine in her stomach and his hand on her breast and her breath was still. They lay down on his narrow bed and Jane thought he had put it in her but then later in the night he rubbed against her back and apologized for coming on her ass. She forgave him, for what she wasn't sure. Spending his sperm outside the vagina. He was probably a good Catholic, or had been once. He was handsome, with a straight nose, very Roman, she thought, a well-shaped mouth, and a strong, athletic body. He had very little hair on his chest, like her father.

They took the subway to work together, Frank talking about his golf game, making polite conversation. All day he eyed her and she eyed him but without desire. When she sold a Barbie doll or a costume she did think, again and again, Well, I'm not a virgin. That was that. Now it's over. Or, now it's begun. These clichés meant as little to her as the sex had. The earth had not moved. She decided that as soon as she stopped working at Macy's she'd stop speaking to Frank.

Jimmy turned over in his bed, the sheets strangling him, and he looked down; he was encased, like a mummy, except for his penis, which lay on top, like a still life. It had been pretty still lately, except for Maurice's sorties down there, which he allowed—permitted, Maurice would put it, nothing is allowed, everything is permitted. Blow jobs were hardly male or female, someone's head down there, if you close your eyes or cover your eyes with your arm, the way Jimmy always did, it could be anyone. He didn't count blow jobs, so it had been still. Kerouac let people give him blow jobs, ending up in bed with men, maybe they did it, maybe they didn't, and wasn't he a man. Or, what was a man. Someone like his father. Someone like his father made love to his mother. Maurice, he smiled to himself, was a much better cook than his mother.

Larry and Marty baked potatoes they called mickeys in fires they'd start near the East River. Their older brother Mike was a tough guy, considerably older, and involved with a fast crowd. "Murder Incorporated," Larry told her, "but because our brother wasn't really a member they left the family alone. There were times when we thought they were waiting for him with guns, but it wasn't true. He just flirted with danger." Mike used to fight with Marty and pin him to the ground, push him around, probably because Marty was

Rose's favorite. He was devoted to Rose—all were—Marty was more embarrassed by the way she looked. It wasn't only that her hair was messier than other mothers'. Rose cut an eccentric figure, wearing big hats and almost stylish coats that had to have a piece of fur around the neck, all seeming to say she belonged somewhere else. She didn't seem to care or notice what people thought. The druggist regularly dispensed to Larry 1,000-cap bottles of Dexamyl, and both he and Jane's father kept their energy going with the help of those capsules. Larry insisted Jane see her father soon, that he missed her, even though he always yelled at her. He was hurt, Larry told her, when she wouldn't let him into her apartment that time after he finished work. But I wasn't expecting him, she told Larry, who declared, But he's your father, he's not any man.

Not any man. He is a man, the first man I knew. He was the only man for all of us, all of us women, wife, girls, daughters. Why had she written the only man for all of us. He is ugly with madness, he is beautiful with his own smell, he is different from us and he comes and goes. He eats breakfast with us. His smile is worth a million bucks. He thinks nothing of himself. Things depend upon his coming and going. He wanted sons. He contents himself with attention. He has ambition and he has no ambition. He hates himself. He hates all of us. He loves himself sometimes, he loves us sometimes. Oh, Daddy.

Chapter 11

Mark said he had nothing to hide because he wasn't afraid of being called unnatural. Grace and he were sitting at the bar and were talking about the play Mark wanted to base on Wilde's "The Birthday of the Infanta." He'd changed his mind; no hospital setting, no nurse. He especially wanted to end with the fairy tale's last line, "For the future let those who come to play with me have no heart." "You've got to have something to hide," Grace said, finishing her beer and lighting a cigarette. They agreed that Wilde was as cruel if not crueler than Poe, because of how the fairy tale begins with the preparations for the Infanta's birthday, and how her birth killed her mother, the beautiful queen, whom the king is still mourning twelve years later. He keeps her embalmed body on display so that he can visit her once a month. "He visits her once a month like his period," Grace laughed.

The cast of characters would include the King, the little Dwarf who doesn't know how ugly he is, and who is brought to the palace to entertain the Infanta, the Infanta, who is the image of her mother, and as cruel as she is beautiful, the flowers who speak and the Infanta's entourage. They can be whoever's in the bar that night, Mark figured, wanting to give the play a kind of lived-in feeling. "Truth, beauty, beauty, truth," he declaimed in the nearly empty bar. It was late afternoon or happy hour. Mark felt there was something really rotten at the bottom of it, and Grace agreed, feeling pretty rotten herself.

You only attack the things that give you trouble, he went on. "Trouble," the woman three barstools from them yelled. "'What do you know about trouble? Trouble is my middle name." Mark peered down the bar, past this woman, to a new face, one covered by a four-day beard that gave it, this nearly ugly face, a handsome aspect, or, at least character. Men can get away with anything Grace thought, watching Mark continuing to look, and then at last walking over to him and pulling up a barstool. Up close his face was both rugged and motherly, or so it seemed to Mark, who forced himself to speak and was answered indifferently by the stranger who didn't look up, as if he couldn't be bothered. "I'm not interested," he said, "I'm into pussy." Mark excused himself, nearly falling off his seat, returning fast to Grace, wondering how he could use that in the play.

Grace told Mark her latest cat dream in which a mother cat has five kittens, very fast, in a big, messy house. The toilet has been pulled out of the bathroom and there's nowhere to piss. A child is sleeping or dead under piles of wet clothes. There's water everywhere and from nowhere to piss they go to "Nowhere to Run," which was arguably the second-best Martha and the Vandellas song, after "Heat Wave." Nowhere to run nowhere to hide and back to hiding and Mark's definition of himself and Grace as demonstration models that would never get bought. Grace said she didn't want to get bought, but wouldn't mind being rented. Mark said he wanted to get married someday and so did she, because deep down there had to be that urge, waiting there like her maternal sell repressed, but ready at any moment to wear white. "Babies," Grace snapped. "You'd be a much better mother than I would." The way Mark saw it, the King would approach the coffin and cry out, as he did in Wilde's story,

"Mi reina, mi reina," then drop to his knees weeping, after covering her embalmed face with kisses, Grace added. That would be the beginning of the play, especially since the King nearly ruined his kingdom on account of his love for her, when she was alive, and perhaps even drove him crazy, his obsession was so great. She died of his excessive demands on her, or so Mark figured, but Grace stressed that the birth of the Infanta killed her, and that's why the King couldn't stand the sight of his beautiful daughter. "Passion brings a terrible blindness upon its servants," Mark quoted, and of course there's the little Dwarf, who has never seen himself at all. And who will die of a broken heart when he does, realizing that the Infanta was only laughing at him.

Mark would've liked to have taken his love and locked him in a room, kept him there, thrown away the key. He would put a line into the King's mouth: "I have set myself in agony upon your strangeness." "Was the Queen strange?" Grace asked. "I don't know," Mark answered, "but it's a play on your highness." "Oh," Grace said, "very funny." Possession is nine-tenths of the law, but would the law cover Mark's keeping his love locked away in a room in Providence. "The law doesn't cover what you want it to cover," he said sullenly.

Grace would be the Infanta and Mark the little Dwarf, although he toyed with playing both the King and the Dwarf. What constituted the most hideous costume and overall design for the Dwarf was under discussion. Something has to be missing. Something has to be hanging from his chin. One of his eyes must be out of the socket or blinded. He would have to have tiny hairy hands without fingernails. Dirty matted hair. Sores, running ones. An enormous nose. Or a face with no nose at all. A head much too large for its pathetic body.

No proportion, Mark would play the Dwarf on his knees, like Jose Ferrer as Toulouse-Lautrec.

The woman who said trouble was her middle name was raging down the end of the bar. "You have a beautiful face, a man loves you. You have a face like a monkey, you only get screwed. Screwed. It's better to be old. You don't care about that. None of that. Can't be fooled anymore." Mark studied Grace's face. "You're pretty, but your nose is a little too big. You're not perfect, there's something just a little bit off about you." He kept studying, and Grace said only Christ was perfect, and she didn't mind. She also didn't mind being called pretty, if she could use it to her advantage, although the advantages were weird. Take the Infanta. Her beauty is almost a trick. And connected to evil. "And your lower lip should be fuller," Mark continued, "the better to beguile." "And you've got too much lip," Grace said, "it makes you lopsided. That's what makes you perfect to play the Dwarf. But imagine if you were really ugly, with a face only a mother could love."

The Infanta never really had a mother, unless you count a woman dying for six months as your mother. Grace thought of Ellen in the mental hospital, and how she didn't really have a mother, either. It was when Ellen called Grace mother that Grace decided to quit that job because, as she told Mark, I'd only end up hurting her. They said goodbye when Ellen was lucid, but Ellen couldn't understand that it was goodbye forever. She touched Grace's hair and for the first time in Grace's life she was moved to sadness for someone else. It made her feel impotent, then angry, that big empty feeling. No one loved her, Ellen, or the Infanta. And it's your right to be mean or crazy, "The King didn't even stay with the Infanta on her birthday," Grace complained. "He was busy taking care of the state," Mark teased. Even though he'd said she wouldn't have to memorize anything, the Infanta's role was growing and Grace was beginning to think that Mark should play it. "I'll never learn it all." "Ah, you're a natural," he said. And she said, "When I hear that word, I want to dye my hair black."

Late at night Grace couldn't memorize her lines and stared into space and then out the space through the window. The empty streets had a ghostliness that was part of night, and there wasn't anything necessarily worse about the night than the day, except for the darkness, which was only natural. The day dyes its hair, too, she thought, that's why it's weird and why I like it, even if it's scary. Under cover of night. The dark. The guy at the bar talking about those murders in Providence. A man stalking women, one after another. Mark and she had been arguing about the end of the Dwarf, his death, and whether or not he had to die, or if it could end differently. Grace said he had to die, and Mark thought maybe he could be put on a respirator and the Infanta forced to confront the consequences of her actions before he died. But then you couldn't use the last line, Grace argued, and that's when the guy at the bar yelled at them about just talking about death like that when real people were being killed, not storybook dwarfs, and who cares anyway, and Mark talked about wanting to give people hope and the guy said he was hopeless, just another artist. "Real murders take place in the real world," he yelled. "What's real?" Mark yelled back. Later in her room Grace wasn't convinced about anything. He said real murder in a menacing way. Real murder committed by real people out there. Out there. "Or even in here," the guy added. Mark was sure he was a cop, undercover, bent on scaring the demimonde. There's épater le bourgeois and there's épater la scum.

Dying of a broken heart is different from being murdered, and she doubted that anyone really died because of love. It seemed so stupid.

After the Dwarf and the Infanta, the flowers had the biggest parts. Carmen, a transsexual, wanted to be either a violet or a tulip, but because of expediency, she would play all the flowers, in one. She can make her own costume, Mark said, anything she wants. "The flowers are vicious little snobs," Carmen said, preparing to recite her lines: "He really is too ugly to be allowed to play anywhere we are." "He should drink poppy juice and go to sleep for a thousand years." "He is a perfect horror, and if he comes near me, I will sting him with my thorns." In Wilde's story the violets don't actually speak but reflect that the Dwarfs ugliness is ostentatious and he would have shown much better taste if he had just looked sad. Carmen said Wilde was right, ugliness does look like misery and Grace said he wasn't saying that. And Mark said he was saying that the reason the Dwarf was despised was because his imperfections made him stand out, and given his lowly origins, he's supposed to be invisible.

It adds up, it doesn't add up. The flowers are snobs, and they're part of nature, but then so is the Dwarf, whom they disdain. Ugliness is kind, beauty is cruel, yet the Dwarf also succumbs to the beauty of the Infanta, because beauty is always beyond reproach, innocent. "Can beauty be innocent and cruel at the same time," Grace wondered aloud to Mark. "Maybe," Mark said, "beauty is as ambiguous as evil and ugliness and innocence." Grace told Mark that she had the feeling that getting old means that you're taken over and forced to forget your innocence. Mark couldn't believe that Grace thought of herself as innocent. She said she wasn't talking about sex, and what had that got to do with innocence anyway. To Grace, innocence meant the time before time counted, when days were long, when summer stretched ahead of you as a real long time and you could do nothing and that was all right. The time she went to summer camp and it seemed like forever. Innocence meant not seeing how ugly things were. Innocence meant that you think of yourself as doing the right thing, even if it looked wrong. Innocence meant you were never going to die and no one you loved would either. Innocence meant you'd never grow old because you could not really be touched. Maybe she meant damaged, she couldn't get damaged. You could still leave, turn away.

"Turn to me," the guy at the bar said. It was the guy who told Mark he was into pussy. He was back, holding racing gloves in one hand, a drink in another. He had all his fingers and he looked dangerous, like the evil hero in a grade B movie. Grace smiled to herself. More like a character actor than a star, and he thought she was smiling at him. Mark had said if she was so into her innocence, maybe she should play the Dwarf. She kept on smiling and talking drunkenly to the stranger. Mark watched them leave. Carmen said that real girls had it much too easy. He took her to a seedy hotel next to the Greyhound Bus Station, and it was all perfect as far as Grace was concerned, except that there was something about him that she couldn't put into words. He stayed here from time to time, he said, when he was in town. His leather jacket was worn, his black pants tight, his hands were large and rough, and he had books on the floor, the kind she wouldn't have expected. Like Nietzsche.

The room was small, with a single electric light bulb hanging from the ceiling, a draft shaking it every once and a while. He had some Jack in the Black in his bag, and they kept on drinking. He didn't seem to notice the place, and Grace supposed he'd seen worse. Maybe everything. When they made love his large hands moved her body around, positioning it finally on a diagonal across the bed. Her body fit into the old mattress as if into a mold. He hardly kissed her and kept repositioning her body into that same spot. Any excitement she had had fled and she went through the motions with him. Neon lights flashed on and off. The glare from crummy signs made it hard to sleep, and Grace woke, dressed fast, and left his room. He called himself Hunter, his last name, he said. She didn't wake him.

Grace repeated this story to Lisa, the singer who worked with the band every other week. "Sounds like a pervert," Lisa said. "A pervert," Mark exclaimed. "Did you ever see *The Naked Kiss*? 'He gave me the naked kiss, the kiss of a pervert.'" "Women are much sweeter," Lisa continued. "Then," Mark went on, "there's that line when he asks her to marry him and he says, 'Our life will be paradise because we are both abnormal.'" Grace ignored Mark as best she could to concentrate on Lisa and the idea of sex with women, at least trying it, and not being able to shake the feeling that being with Hunter was like being with a ghost. She didn't think he came either, not that it really mattered.

Time, actually the sundial, is taken aback by the Dwarf. But the birds like him because he used to feed them in the forest. The flowers think the birds are awful because well-bred people always stay in the same place, like themselves, they say. And the lizards are tolerant of him. Mark called them humanists. Mark wanted to make the scene in which the Dwarf remembers the forest as paradisaical as possible, given the restrictions of the bar, of course. The forest is his Eden, before his fall, his look into the mirror. That's everyone's fall, Grace thought. Grace and Mark couldn't remember the first time they'd looked into mirrors, and wondered what they'd thought. Little kids see themselves for the first time and somehow figure out that that creature is themselves. The Dwarfs long walk through the palace seeking the Infanta leads him to find himself in the mirror. He finally realizes it's himself because he's carrying the rose she gave him after he had performed for her. But the Dwarf is too horrified by his image, just like the flowers. Was his image of himself perfect? Then he sees it's not true. Grace said she was reminded of when her mother thought she was old enough to be left alone at night and told her that now she was her own baby-sitter. "What's that got to do with this?" Mark asked. Grace said she didn't know, it just came to mind.

They were at a party and Grace was thinking about ugliness, beauty, and anarchy, then found herself talking to, or listening to, an ugly guy who was telling her his life story. "I started going to therapy after I shot my best friend. We were living in California, and he was driving me crazy. It was going on for two years, so finally I shot him." The funny thing was that the guy, his best friend, didn't press charges, because they were best friends, and he didn't go to jail or even court. That anyway was what Grace found most weird. The ugly guy said he had moved first to New York, then here, and didn't think his friend would ever find him again. "Sometimes I miss him."

He wasn't a monster, and she didn't feel revolted, but Grace walked away, the way you can do at parties, right after some admission has been made that's intimate. Leave someone in mid-sentence. Or your eyes and their eyes are always revolving, scanning. You move in and out. Anyway, Grace did. A beautiful woman talked to her about decadence. She said she couldn't afford to be decadent. She had children and people without children just couldn't understand, and she wasn't blaming them either, couldn't understand what it meant. "Because I have children, I can only look at it, I can't be it. I realized that people don't have time to look at things, so I started shouting. Just to be heard. I want to make a path for my children, someplace in the future where they can live, so I have to shout." It turned out that she was married to the ugly guy who had shot his best friend years ago. The woman said her husband had a tendency to exaggerate. The woman was shouting to be heard in the crowded room and Grace and she were united in their interest in a couple across the room who were commanding attention. They paced back and forth, along the edge of the room. She would stand and stare, glare, significantly in his direction, while he assumed a pose of indifference. Then she'd move away sullenly and dance back. They acted as if they didn't know each other, and as if they didn't know where the other stood, so that in some way they needed to find each other but were thwarted. "Exhausting, isn't it?" said the shouting woman with children. Mark said they were like poisonous snakes, charged with current. "People like that enliven a party," he continued, "especially such a straight one." But Grace was watching two women dancing together, oblivious that they were the only ones dancing. Grace asked Lisa about her life and how she knew she was gay.

Lisa said she'd been best friends with this girl for a year when one afternoon it just happened. She was sitting on her lap, fooling around, and suddenly they were kissing passionately. Lisa said she had on her rosary and her girlfriend ripped it from her neck and threw it bead by bead across the room. "'That rosary meant so much to me," Lisa said, who had picked up all the beads from the floor and put them in an envelope, to save. Lisa said the other girl didn't want it to go on because she already had a girlfriend, but Lisa said she didn't care and spent weekends with her until she was totally fed up. "She told me I was too dependent, but that started me out. Men didn't seem so necessary anymore, and the sex with women is much more beautiful. Men are abrasive, if you know what I mean." Lisa said her parents were in the Midwest, her mother drinking up a storm, a typical suburban housewife, her father a typical businessman, except that somehow he never could earn any money. "Both of them love their afternoon martini. A little olive, a little onion, sitting on the couch. I suppose I was sheltered, except that my mother was an ugly drunk. When I went home the last time my mother called me a lesbian and slapped me in the face, and I looked at her real calmly and said, 'You've seen the last of me.' I suppose it's sad, but I don't have anything to say to them anyway. I think they regret having sent me to college."

Grace flirted outrageously with Lisa, who seemed to have a lot of patience and one night patience was rewarded. Lisa took Grace home and Grace lost her virginity yet again. It was different, and Grace was at a loss. She worried that she wasn't doing it right. Later it induced in her a state of psychic weightlessness that made her giddy with possibility. She floated on that for days. She told Mark that she didn't know if she was gay or not, but she didn't think she cared. A man's mouth, a woman's mouth, some things felt the same, other things were different. She felt like a twelve-year-old and like Mata Hari. Lisa's body. Her own. She couldn't explain any of it to Mark. She wished men had breasts. She told him that she was worried about the etiquette with women. Would she have to be nicer to Lisa than to the guys she slept with.

Mark was peculiar about her relationship with Lisa and Lisa said it was because he couldn't enter into it the way he could when Grace fucked some guy. Then he could be the guy she was fucking or Grace. And everyone wants to know how women do it. She told Mark what Lisa said and that he seemed upset at her bisexuality. He said he wasn't, that bisexuals were failed homosexuals and he told her she was too young to fail. What was failure, she wanted to know. Finally he relented and announced that this was her grace period but after a while she'd have to make up her mind. He said he didn't mean just sex.

Make up her mind, her face. Dress it up, rearrange the pieces, move the furniture, change the decor. The design. I'd like a few more angles on that part of my mind. Remove the frills. She felt she was up for grabs, even to herself. It was as difficult to know what to fill her days with as her body, or mind. It wasn't like learning the alphabet; it was more like unlearning it, not taking it in and not spitting it out. I know it by heart, she thought about a movie she had seen a million times. There was something reassuring in having the same responses to a movie she knew inside out. Repetition was like a visit to her family, except she never went home. Repetition like living at home. Her visits to already seen films produced familiar sights, cries, rushes of blood, melancholy. It was always the same. A home away from home, these responses. Automatic responses. Like moving her hand to Lisa's breast. Or had she learned that in the movies, or at her mother's breast. Except she'd always hated her mother's body. When Ruth took off her longline bra, and her breasts fell from those white cotton cups, flat and sagging, like her life, Grace thought, exactly the life she didn't want, contained in that body. Always the white cotton full slip under her clothes. And the girdle that mercilessly controlled her figure, which, after two children, had spread and about which she didn't do anything. Her mother's heavy arms extending from a serviceable housedress. And when she took it off she turned from her daughter, as if ashamed or embarrassed. Grace had never seen her mother's cunt, that part of her mother's body was entirely forbidden from her view, and it was that part she wanted revealed. It seemed impossible that she hadn't seen it, but she couldn't remember it, the way she did remember her mother's breasts, as if the upper part of a woman was all right to show, but not the lower part, and later when Grace stole girlie magazines from candy stores, there too only the breasts were exposed, but those breasts were bouncy and taut, not at all like her mother's, and maybe that's why her mother was ashamed in front of her. Or that's what Grace thought sitting in suspense at the edge of her mother's bed, waiting for her mother to show herself to her only daughter, her baby, as she called Grace when they were alone together.

Lisa called her baby too, but Lisa and her mother were worlds apart. Lisa was always aware of the audience, and her effect on it, and Grace liked to watch her work the crowd, as Lisa put it, her long thin arms dangling at her sides or moving fast with the music. Mark made some more cynical comments about love between women and Grace said his true colors were showing, to which he replied that at least he had true colors, as if Grace didn't. Another murder had been committed the night before and Grace couldn't sleep, wondering if evil really did exist. Lisa had told her that she flirted with danger but wouldn't know evil if it came up and shook her. Grace said that was because it didn't exist except as absence, and Lisa laughed and said something about lapsed Catholics being all the same. Later Grace remembered also asking her mother if evil existed and getting the answer she'd given to Lisa. She had problems, she complained to Mark, who complained to her that the play had its problems too, although it takes a kind of leap in perspective to anthropomorphize art like that. It was as if the play were already there, and all he had to do was find it.

Mark might have the Infanta dress like her dead mother, but first he had to establish the mother's costume and appearance, and that meant a portrait, or something or someone in the open coffin on display while the play went on. Also he wanted the Infanta to show, in some way, that she too was wounded, damaged, and that even though beautiful, she like the Dwarf was imperfect. Grace refused to plead for the King's love, saying it was out of character and Mark countered that it was more out of character for Grace than the Infanta, and the two of them fought again, Mark bringing it to a close by suggesting that they were both tired and Grace was, after all, his star.

There were no stars out that night as Grace wrote Celia that she was having an affair with a woman, but still sleeping with men, to which Celia replied in her next letter that Grace might be having the best of all possible worlds. Grace answered, finally, that she didn't think there was a best and she told Celia that she didn't want to feel responsible to anybody. She felt that Lisa was getting more involved with her, and Grace wasn't sure what she wanted, although she liked Lisa a lot. "I'm not getting married to anyone," she wrote Celia, "whatever Mark thinks about my natural urges."

Mark had taken to dressing like Wilde during rehearsals, and had just read *De Profundis*, which caused him to cry and exclaim that at least they wouldn't go to jail for their unnatural acts, and that Wilde had died for their sins, and Grace told him he was making her sick. She grabbed a bunch of her hair, looked at it, with its split ends, and thought she should go visit Ellen soon or sometime because it nagged at her, Ellen sitting forever in that bin, with no possible future. She split each hair from one end to the other, staring at the strand of hair with terrific concentration, her lips pursed, her eyes nearly crossed. She sat like that for hours rerunning the day's events. She thought Lisa was acting weird. Maybe she was tired of her, or maybe she was just tired, or maybe Grace herself was tired, or didn't know Lisa well enough to be able to tell. If you ever could tell those things about someone else. Where did her thoughts leave off and Lisa's begin anyway? Love is like that Mark would say if he were sitting on the edge of her bed consoling her or cajoling her, both somewhat the same to her these days. But she wasn't sure she was in love with Lisa, whatever that was. She didn't expect it, encourage it, or even, she was sure, really want it. Not yet. Love could wait. She'd grow into it like a pair of pants a size too big. Grace thought her time in bars would lead to something, but Lisa said she shouldn't expect anything to lead to anything. And she told Grace she didn't want to be her baby-sitter. Grace ignored Lisa for the rest of the night, but now she reviewed the conversation along her split ends.

Grace told Mark that she hadn't slept at all and that she felt she was filling up, and one day she might spill over. She was a story. There was hers, Mark's, Lisa's, the play, the people at the bar, hundreds of stories. Mark asked her to concentrate on her role, forget everything but it for just a few days, until D-Day, then he said he could talk to her about how she was in a story and so was he. Not in one, she said, we are them.

Her role: innocent and evil, physically beautiful and spiritually ugly, powerful and powerless. Grace told him she'd act the lines, but if he expected her to know how to be all that, he was crazy. "I am crazy," he answered, "and so are you." On the night of the run-through that guy was in the audience, the one who gave Grace the creeps and at the same time was fascinating, like a horror movie. Lisa watched, watched Grace's eyes find his, and didn't think she wanted to live through another of Grace's adventures. Especially this one. Lisa told Grace she was going out of town for a while, the gig bored her, and she'd return after both of them had put enough between them that neither would mind just being friends. Grace was indignant, as Lisa thought she'd be, told her she didn't want to be friends with her, and that she really didn't care anyway. Grace knew that Lisa would expect her to get over it. Pretty fast and probably in the arms of another. Probably a man. And if it was going to be that creep, Lisa had told Grace, she didn't want to see it. She'd seen enough already. Straight women were a pain in the ass. Or like quicksand was how she put it to Grace. Lisa liked being the one to go, to move on, to get back on the road.

Grace had imagined that Lisa would always be around. She consoled herself by thinking that she probably wasn't a lesbian anyway. Misquoting a line from *Trash*, Mark told her she wasn't a good lesbian but, as Grace herself had once said, no one is perfect.

She wanted to forget and she threw herself into her part. Now that she'd been abandoned, her heart supposedly broken, she did feel a little tragic, or at least wounded, the way Mark said he wanted the Infanta to be, not just a monster. The creepy guy hanging around was a distraction. She didn't imagine that she could do anything to him that would touch him or anger him or move him or move him away as she thought she'd done with Lisa, and in an odd way he was safe. At least she didn't feel like killing herself, not for somebody else. If she ever did it, she told Mark, it would be only because of herself. Mark said that was wonderfully selfish and this mood was perfect for the Infanta. In rehearsal Grace recited her last line with real fury: "For the future let those who come to play with me have no heart." Then she stormed off the stage, not at all like a princess, or Mark's idea of a princess. Still, Mark was pleased that she had assumed her role. Even though she said that she didn't like the Infanta because she didn't do anything, and why, she asked Mark, do people write stories about people who don't do anything. At least the Dwarf was an entertainer, not like the Infanta or the King, who didn't have to earn anyone's attention.

Chet Baker singing "They're writing songs of love but not for me," Mark decided, was the right touch for the fade-out. The Dwarf is lying dead, stage right, and the Infanta has made her final exit. The record was a gift from Bill to Grace after she'd broken his heart. Perfect, Mark thought. Perfect too was the enlarged reproduction of Holbein's *Dance of Death* , which figured in the fairy tale and was part of the spare scenery, even more apparent or obvious with only the dead Dwarf, Mark himself, lying there onstage. Too bad he couldn't see it, and though he had Grace stand in, or lie in, for him a couple of times, it wasn't the same. They were nearly ready for opening night, as much as you could call a first night at Oscar's an opening. And when that night came, the guy was waiting backstage, so to speak, as if he knew something that Grace didn't, and after she spoke her last line, again in fury she defiantly walked over to him and into his waiting arms, so to speak, feeling that there was nothing to lose.

Chapter 12

Emily awoke from this dream. Someone like her is enticed into a room whose walls are deep red. Like shame, she thinks later. She is given a seat by a man smoking a cigar.

Then there are many men. All of them want her, whoever she is. Want her very much. They're willing to give her anything. Anything at all. She says she's not interested in money, that she wants to be respected. One man spits into a silver spittoon. Her hands are bound behind her. She's not going to get anything. She's made a mistake of some sort and can't correct it. One by one the men lift her dress, although she thought she was wearing pants, they lift her dress and fuck her. She is taken over and over again. She does not resist. The dream disgusts her although she thinks she has had an orgasm in her sleep. Emily wonders how women can know, if their dreams aren't wet like men's. One should not be fooled by the surface of things, as that surface is easily broken and disrupted. As Emily's mother remarked to her once, "Don't things get dirty easily?"

What Emily read she became, identifying with the hero or heroine, the protagonist or the ideas, much as she did when she watched movies and cried. To this becoming her dictionary was a map, and learning new words was like leaving home. A map picked at indiscriminately. "Pastiche...hodgepodge." "Passionate...easily aroused to anger; capable of intense feeling; see ardent, fervid, fervent."

"Imperialism…the policy, practice, or advocacy of extending power and dominion of a nation…" Looking up words she knew or thought she knew reassured her. Finding out that she was wrong scared her. Any sort of discovery, especially of contradiction, satisfied her. Her men's army pants had shredded at the inner thigh and, unable to sew, she took an old T-shirt, cut a swatch, and sewed it badly to the crotch and down the inner leg. It looked more like a bandage than a patch but the hole was covered. She flipped to the back of the dictionary. "Vicarious…serving instead of someone or something else; in the existence of another." She liked that phrase. "Victualler…the keeper of a tavern." "Violence…an exertion of physical force; outrage; fervor." "Virago…a woman of great stature; a loud, overbearing woman." "Virtuoso…one who excels." Passionate, fervid; violence, fervor. She repeated fervid a few times, thought about having a fever, then looked up furtive. It seemed to her that there should have been more connection between passion and stealth, but there wasn't. She was dissatisfied but did not feel her worst, which was reserved for those times when she felt there was nothing to say at all.

It is a strange experience for whoever regards himself as the One to be revealed to himself as otherness, alterity.

Christine told Emily she had an intelligent face and Emily answered that she could fool people with makeup, but it was difficult to keep up appearances. Emily was reading *The Second Sex*, and Christine, *Memoirs of a Dutiful Daughter*. De Beauvoir's discussion of narcissism, her comments on makeup, the subject of their discussion. "In a woman dressed and adorned, nature is present but under restraint by human will remolded near to man's desire." If you look up desire in the dictionary, Emily said, it says that it's an impulse, a conscious one, toward something that promises satisfaction in its attainment. Christine thought that sounded too clinical. And Emily said she resented having to do anything about her appearance, that when she put on makeup she felt like she was giving in. Christine said she couldn't stand the way she looked without makeup, and that Emily needed to be more narcissistic. When she was with a man she slept with her makeup on, she told Emily. The man's desire. Emily asked, "Even your false eyelashes? What if one fell off in the middle of the night?" "I always get up before he does," Christine said. At their local bar they invented the term facial imperialism, while they watched couples from a small table. They talked about school. Edith. De Beauvoir and Sartre. Emily watched herself, careful not to say the wrong thing to Christine, who she thought misinterpreted easily. She peered at Christine's face closely. Emily squinted, causing Christine to think she was upset. She didn't like the way Christine told her what to do when she wasn't asked. She hated her makeup, thought it made her look like a doll. Emily told herself that if Christine wanted to look like a doll, that was her business. Christine watched Emily's face, its blankness masking what Christine knew to be anger, based, she felt, on jealousy. Emily smiled and said, If you want me to I'll take your books back to Forty-second Street when I go. Then they both smiled, and Emily hated herself.

I knew that she thought much less of me than I thought of her. Emily felt better sitting in front of her typewriter than in that bar, and plunged into her paper on Puritanism. The Puritans were dissatisfied in England and the English Church was dissatisfied with them. America was to be their Holy Kingdom. But because of the schizophrenic quality of their tenets, the Puritans worked feverishly without hope.

(Or should that be doubled-edged quality? and worked fervently?) Hopelessness, the riverbed of the American drive for material wealth. Hopelessness was at the bottom of everything. Sin was inevitable. No one ever knew if they were of the elect. In a new world, one without tradition or order, the Puritan work ethic could be the driving force for the new settlers, throwing them into a frenzy. How to show their goodness, their saintliness? It follows that paranoia and materialism walk hand in hand (does that really follow?). And fame will become the visible proof of God's love or approval.

Professor Wilson would want her to back up these statements with proof. Can anything be proved? Maybe all you can do is pretend you don't have to. Emily Dickinson turned away from that society, shut herself off from it. She wasn't trying to be seen to be doing good. She was either a lesbian or in love with a married man. And then she retired. Dickinson used that word somewhere. "Retire…to withdraw from action or danger." I wish I'd been a transcendentalist. She pictured a cottage in the country. Behind it was a forest, a small animal darting around the trees. This kind of image requires sun, and it was sunny where the giant trees weren't blocking it. There was a stream too, and sometimes she'd see herself in a large flowered bonnet, wading in the water. There'd be a gruff voice or two in the background. She wouldn't be entirely alone. Keith rang the buzzer; it was midnight. He was wearing black shades and a leather band around his wrist. Emily threw on her army pants and fervently hoped that the patch wouldn't descend during the night. They went out. What have you been doing? Why are you in such a crummy mood? Do you want to have a meal or not? Let's go back to your place. I like it here. I don't know. I think it's kind of weird this way. We're a hodge-podge. Oh,

Emily, he whispered into her ear, we're both too weird, that's all. He bit her on the neck, and the cabdriver took them back to her place. He wouldn't tell her if he was in love with anyone else, and besides, he said, why should it matter. He told her she had beautiful breasts and fell asleep.

A naive young girl is caught by the gleam of virility; what she always wants is for her lover to represent the essence of manhood.

She is at a party and she is the only girl. She assumes there are other girls somewhere, but she cannot see them. There are birthday decorations on the ceiling and walls; she is fourteen. The boys call her by another name. She is not Emily. They ask her if she wants to do it and she says yes. They tie her hands behind her, just in case, one says, and in the corner of this basement, each boy fucks her.

She slept and felt she hadn't, woke, saw Keith on the floor, feel back to sleep as if it were her lover. When they did wake up he played another tape for her and asked her what she thought. She didn't know. It was all right. His eyes were big and black, his lower lip fuller than his upper lip. It's okay, she said again. He stood and walked to the bathroom at the edge of her small room and stretched. For a moment she thought he did that deliberately, to entice her. But she wasn't, and whatever she did feel for him wasn't what he or Christine thought. She had no desire for him. The idea itself infuriated her and she hated Christine for thinking it. He pulled his T-shirt down, over his head, and with his head covered she stared at his nipples, which were brown and wide with a few black hairs growing from them. His strong arms didn't fit his image of waste, decay, and his skin was so pale, she thought of Hilda. So pale and unblemished it appeared indifferent to pain, unused to needles. The other guy was getting more attention than he was. It's the singer-not-the-song kind of discussion. Emily sat coiled up on her skinny bed, her arms wrapped around her, then he left.

This morbid daydreaming was of a kind to assuage the narcissism of the young girl who feels life inadequate and fears to face the realities of existence.

Christine decided that if Emily escaped less into dreams, into literature, and even history, she might have a more active and glamorous life. Christine had pored over the pages of *Vogue* well enough to know what was right and wrong with her own face. And she had fashioned herself, had even, since a child, planned her dreams so as not to be disappointed. I was always efficient, she thought. The water was boiling for tea and she thought about Emily and why Emily hadn't called yesterday and it was almost noon and still no call today. She phoned her. Emily was asleep but said she wasn't. She said she was only thinking. Emily didn't like to be caught in the act. Christine pulled her robe to her, put an egg up to boil, opened a book. Merleau-Ponty: "Consciousness always exists in a situation." It took a lot of effort not to think about Emily and what Emily might be thinking about her. They were so different from each other.

Christine threw aside bad thoughts and imagined herself in a neutral space where she was safe. Her long thin body needed a lot of space, a design of her own. She knew how to take care of herself. Her mother had insisted she learn all the womanly skills, had taught her them in fact with an urgency that Christine still felt. She would always be able to support herself, she told herself. If a man wouldn't marry her. This last thought was not enunciated, it was a breath that was not breathed. She remembered watching *Queen for a Day* and, feeling embarrassed for the women, crying when the one she thought should win didn't. Often they were married women with disabled husbands, otherwise they wouldn't have been on the show. Emily still hadn't called her back. Maybe she was angry at her about what she said about Keith. Emily didn't know anything about men. On the other hand she said she didn't care. Christine didn't want to have another fight with Emily, after which she withdrew and Christine felt as rejected as she did now. The egg was too soft; she liked her eggs just right and didn't time them. Christine stared at the book, then the phone. It might become animated through her need. She wished she could ask Emily if she thought there was a difference between need and desire, but maybe later. Christine threw down the philosophy book and picked up *Memoirs of a Dutiful Daughter*, which, at any point, could bring her to tears.

That was what was wrong; I needed Zaza.

Now Emily hated her paper, her poems. She could hear Edith outside the door, there was a sound in those movements that meant she might want company, but Emily couldn't provide it. If she could rouse herself she'd go see a double feature, anything. Suddenly she jumped off the bed and resolutely moved to her typewriter, the one that her mother had given her when she was thirteen. You're the one with talent, her mother had said, handing over the machine she had hoped to write her own novel on. Yet Emily had never been eager to show her mother what she came up with on that machine and Emily's mother felt overlooked, slighted. Emily started writing a story in the first person. I am almost as angry with my girlfriend as I am with my boyfriend and I don't know why. I don't know why I like Keith when he doesn't like me. She crossed that out. He doesn't say he likes me but seems to like me. I want this story to be about independence and dependence. Keith and Christine will be the central characters and the story will revolve around their demands on me, Emily, and how Emily thinks she doesn't need or want them, but somehow is completely entangled with them. Against my will, she wrote. She thought she'd have to disguise the characters completely so that Keith and Christine wouldn't recognize themselves, but the story would be mangled if she did, and then what was the point. It seemed like another demand they were making of her.

Real conflicts arise when the girl grows older; as we have seen, she wished to establish her independence from her mother.

This was a story not a poem. Emily could use dialogue, direct argument between Christine and herself. But Emily wasn't sure she knew what the argument was. Sometimes she thought that if Christine asked her for one more favor, she'd strangle her. Then she hated herself. Christine shouldn't ask her so then she wouldn't have to be put in that position. Anyway, she couldn't say no. But there wasn't a story, there's no plot in what's not there. So much seemed not to be there, and yet normally she was very articulate, able to express herself with language, language her best ally when it wasn't her worst enemy. Like now. What did Christine want from her or want in general. Who is Christine, she wrote, and felt disgusted. The unexpressed is stronger than the expressed, it must be, she thought. She looked up ineffable and wrote, My relationship with Christine skirts the ineffable. Except Emily didn't wear skirts and why should she write about women who did? Could she use that figure of speech when it represented another kind of woman? Or, which woman was she writing about? Anyway, the thing didn't have a plot, no drama, didn't build or go anywhere. Emily comforted herself with the idea that plots were like skirts, you either did or you didn't use things like that. Why do people want stories to go somewhere, she asked herself, and retired to bed.

In a well-regulated human heart friendship occupies an honorable position, but it has neither the mysterious splendor of love, nor the sacred dignity of filial devotion. And I never called this hierarchy into question.

Over Christine's bed was an old photograph. It was torn from a book and much cherished by her. Two adolescent girls are in party dresses. They are playing blind man's buff. One of the girls is standing at the side of the door, in the foreground. The other, blindfolded, is coming forward, one hand out in front of her, reaching, the other arm quiet at her side. She's reaching and bent forward, as if misshapen by her ambition. She's in a white dress that's down to the floor, although the neckline is cut lower than one might expect for the period and her age. The other girl, the one who watches has drawn back her black dress, just slightly. There's sunlight behind them. It's a romantic image, poignant and eerie. The eerie quality is what made the photograph perfect. Christine wondered if everything romantic was eerie, unnerving, because of how it always ends. The girl who is blindfolded seems like she doesn't know that, is innocent in white, while the girl in black, her hand cautiously holding her skirt, eyes wide open and looking, appears to know what the other doesn't. The future is the foreground. When she made love to men below that picture, Christine held that irony inside her. Her efficiency did not extend to, in fact was circumvented by, her relations with men. Just what, she laughed to Emily, do they really want? Emily wanted a copy of the picture, but Christine didn't want her to have it. It was enough that they borrowed each other's clothes and books. I have to have some things for myself, Christine thought.

This time the dream Emily told no one was set in the American West. The girl who was and was not Emily—it she says, adamantly, You've got me wrong, I'm not Emily—is wearing a bright red dress, very long, trailing on the floor behind her. The red dress is cut perfectly to her perfect body and one by one the men lift that long red dress and enter her. Her arms and legs are tied.

Woman is offered inducements to complicity.

Christine is driving me crazy, Emily thought after waking up with trouble from that dream. She always makes me feel I've done the wrong thing. I can never please her. She's more beautiful. I can't trust her. Yet she felt she had no reason not to trust her. These thoughts weren't exactly thoughts. Emily didn't want Christine to meet Keith. She decided they would fall in love and then she would have to stop speaking to both of them. She pictured the scene: walking in on them in flagrante. Christine jumps up and runs toward her, while Keith manages his embarrassment by lighting a cigarette almost casually. These kinds of thoughts were intrusions that Emily felt were willed by forces outside her. Hers and not hers. Just like the dirty dreams. The line between fantasy and reality can be walked like a tightrope, and often Emily could not read between the lines. It made reading Kafka effortless, things just as they are. She felt that both of them were realists because they didn't have to distinguish between kinds of experience. Of course she recognized herself as a paranoid and it made her feel modern and better adjusted to whatever was to come. Her story about herself, Keith, and Christine continued: the two girls were looking at each other in the mirror, so that to the other there were two images to see, the real and the reverse image of the real. Each girl spoke to the mirror image, in reverse, and the person in front of that reflection. They had a normal conversation, but inside the person and beneath the image there was the reverse, mirrored by the mirror. The reverse was apparent to the other, and not the self. Emily thought that whatever she was thinking, Christine might be thinking too.

Papa used to say with pride: Simone has a man's brain; she thinks like a man; she is a man. And yet everyone treated me like a girl.

When Emily returned to making notes for her paper, it was a relief. The Puritans were in Vietnam, another holy mission, all for their, the other's, good. Of course it had to do with money—, she wrote, hearing the word in syllables—in the heartland, they're not thinking about money, they're thinking about God and doing right, evil Commies. She'd have to clean up this paper and put it in the right language. If I ever graduate, she thought, it's because I'll have agreed to this language. She still couldn't tell if she was learning anything. That's why it took her forever to finish one of these papers. That should be obvious, she thought. It surprised her why things were obvious to her and not to someone else. Christine and she were not really surprised by each other's connections. But she couldn't bring herself to tell Christine about her dreams. Emily had read that in England people who had seen the Loch Ness monster called themselves experienced monster-watchers. You can't restrain your monsters all the time, they slip out, awkward, angry, and ugly, to embarrass and humiliate. Emily got humiliated as fast as she got red under a hot sun. She turned pale when she'd made a mistake, let something slip, and felt really dead from embarrassment. Those little deaths—the one she hadn't experienced in sex—had experienced through mistakes, errors, flaws. She tried to observe herself, to contain that which might reveal too much. She could see a kind of parallel between her containment policy and those global efforts on the part of her government, but to bring that into her paper would be another line of thought again.

Keith phoned just as she wrote, Fame and paranoia are transformations, convoluted forms of salvation and sainthood. I think I can prove that, she muttered as she picked up the receiver. Their record was selling, but he didn't have any money. Puritans wanted to conform and have the world conform to their idea of what God would want. Keith kept talking and she kept writing, pausing only to say that she'd have dinner with him and could lend him some money, if he'd pay her back soon. Perhaps if she wore a long red dress. She hated that thought almost as much as Christine hated feeling undressed no matter what she wore. Not exactly undressed, but raw. Like an uncooked egg. Christine's soft-boiled egg had been much too runny, and she ate it with annoyance. When she was a child her mother would put pieces of bread into a soft egg, so that the yellow was almost soaked up and she could eat it. Christine couldn't bring herself to do it, baby herself that way. Life without mother had to be categorically different from life with mother. She had just spoken with her mother, who had again asked for a raise and then in anger put her eyeglasses on upside down. They laughed about it, her mother's ineptitude, and it would be a good story to repeat to Emily. Emily, she thought, would love it.

Part V

Chapter 13

What shall Cordelia speak? Love and be silent.

Cordelia loved King Lear as much as Jane loved her father, but Cordelia was a better daughter. He kicked her out and she came to his rescue. Jane didn't think she wanted to rescue her father, even if she could. Jane had two older sisters, also. One said to her, I like you better when you're fat. You're nicer. Jane didn't think of herself as nice, and began to refer to herself as she when making entries in her diary. Jimmy told her that when she died he'd publish them and everyone would cry because she was dead. Jane didn't want them published. The thought of it made her sick.

She is a player in his world. It is good and evil, and he tells her she's evil. He also tells her he loves her. She's four years old and she's hiding in the bathroom. She made him angry. She did something to make Frank angry. Jane scratched that out. She didn't want Frank in her diary anymore. She didn't have to see him because she was back in college. She felt lucky to have met Maria, someone to talk to. Jane went to the phone and dialed her number, but it was busy. She arouses the devil in him. She arouses in him the devil. Lois would've liked being in college, she would've gotten something out of it. She is passing time or is suspended in it. In the front of Jane's very first diary was a picture of her dead friend, taken when they were ten, at a party when they barely knew each other. Lois is grinning, no idea of death, nothing like this shows no matter how long one stares. Maurice had once quoted Duchamp: "After all it is always the other person who dies." Jane forgot who wrote it, but her imperfect memory had recorded that this appeared on somebody's tombstone. Maurice told Jimmy he was sick of her imperfections.

Jane wasn't perfect, as Felix predicted she might be. Even with sex. Though now that she wasn't innocent of it and not considered innocent, life was different. It was as if a door had been opened and once it was open, it couldn't be shut. You know that old worry that they can tell you're not a virgin, that it shows. It does. But not on your face. It's in your body, out of your body, and it's in your mind. She had been entered.

Jane fell in love with a guy who lived with someone else and told her they were breaking up. He moves toward her and she feels something never felt before. A shudder. He's tall and sandy-haired. They're introduced while watching a fire on St. Mark's Place. It's a wonderful way to meet, they agree. They walk away, toward the west. She takes two steps to his one. They sit opposite each other in an old diner with booths and a great jukebox. She's never felt this way before and she thinks it's the real thing. She decides not to sleep with him until some time passes. Then it'll be right, it'll mean more. It's a kind of empty terrain she feels herself in: pale eyes, long legs, the shudder, the sense of being looked at nourishing her. This shifts into her being swallowed, taken in through the eye and the mouth, devoured without being touched. She swallows longing.

We have this hour a constant will to publish our daughter's several dowers, so that future strife may be prevented now.

Uncle Larry wanted to see Jane. Business was so bad he and her father were trying to sell, if they could find a buyer. Both men had wanted to leave the business to their children, all girls. The eldest sister wondered what would have happened had there been a boy. But as it was, all girls, and nothing to inherit. Larry and Jane were walking in Central Park, heading for the cafeteria and frankfurters and milk, to feed Larry's ulcer. He was talking about how it was in the office, with no customers. Just bolts of material around, neatly stacked and colorful. The salesmen had been let go, then one died of a heart attack. She pictured her father, bent over a piece of fabric, the magnifying glass to his eye. "We just walk around the office or look at each other. Sometimes that Filipino comes in with his pretty wife, but we don't have anything to sell him. He's polite and leaves and your father gets humiliated and I try to cheer him up. He takes everything so hard." The monkeys jumped, the gorilla stared, and the orangutan and her child sat in a corner, picking bugs from each other. "You always forget," Larry said, "how ugly zoos are until you see them again. Kids see animals on television, they don't need to see real ones." The seals were being fed. They were leaping out of the water, grabbing a fish from the keeper's hand, diving back down again, all one continuous movement, clean and deliberate. Larry thought that the seals looked all right. Small children squealed each time a seal rose out of the water, a miracle. A child was crying and Jane watched her. Her mother had walked away, leaving her with another child who was slightly older. As soon as the mother's hand had left hers, the child screamed. Her face got red and her eyes rolled around. She screamed and screamed and screamed. Jane watched. She was angry at the child for screaming. It had done something wrong. It was being too demanding. It deserved it. Why couldn't she leave her mother alone? Jane wondered if you could scream and breathe at the same time. Watching, she felt suspended in it. It was like being at and in the movies simultaneously. "We haven't looked at the home movies lately," she said to Larry when the mother came back to the child. Larry asked her if she was remembering the first time they took her here. "Sort of," Jane answered.

Jane was the keeper of the family home movies. She'd watched them by herself when she was no more than seven. Getting out the 8mm projector, setting it up, making the room dark. The family before she was born. The family after she was born. Everyone running toward the camera when Daddy yelled action. Daddy said he liked to get movement into everything. The trip to West Point before she was born. The trip to Canada when she was eight. The sister, as an adolescent, who hates being photographed. That sister, a baby, a cherub who smiles at the camera, Daddy. The other sister crying, sunlight on her shiny hair. She sits in a stuffed chair, mostly in shadow, tears running down her face, her red mouth loose with fatigue. The fight between sister and Mom. Mom waving the camera away, jerking her head to the side. Daddy tan from a trip he made alone to Bermuda when Mom was pregnant with her. Shots of that pregnancy. She lumbers slowly toward the camera, her daughters running to her side, jumping in front of her. They're small and active, she's big, her movement contained, labored. When slowed down the movements and gestures will of course reveal more, as if Proust had his hand in it and not just technology. Jane doesn't slow down the projector when she's a little girl. At full speed she watched herself, six months old, being given the bottle by

Mom, who's looking at the camera, Daddy, so that the bottle doesn't go into Jane's mouth but waves near it.

She sees him for two weeks. Nearly three weeks. Jane moves the coffee cup to her mouth and remembers his eyes above his coffee cup. The other woman he's with is older than she is and older than him. He's an actor and in a play and for two weeks she walks him to his rehearsals and watches him disappear behind a wooden door. She won't sleep with him until everything is right and he's left the woman. He kisses her and swings her in the air. Jane is pretending the brim of the cup is his mouth touching her mouth. She watches him move his leg. His leg touches hers as his lips touch hers. Words come out of his mouth. He tells her he loves her and that he'll always love her. She wants his words to be physical. The scene repeats. He moves his leg, he kisses her, he loves her. Jane tells Maria about him and Maria laughs. "You believe that line. You middle-class girls. Jesus." Jane wants to walk away from her friend and sit alone in the cafeteria, but she doesn't. She drinks more coffee and they talk about *King Lear*. Jane said in class that Lear wanted Cordelia sexually and the girl in front of her turned, her hand raised, as if to hit her. The teacher, a man, intervened. "Now, now," he said. "Now, now, girls." But she didn't give her father what he wanted. She didn't say what he wanted to hear, that she'd love him more than anyone, even her husband. "Cordelia's a goody-goody," Maria said, watching Jane's reaction. "I like Regan and Goneril.'" "But they're horrible," Jane said. "Lear must've done something to them. Goneril says,'He may hold our lives in mercy.' Remember? They were scared of him." "Why wasn't Cordelia?" "She believed him," Maria answered.

Safer than trust too far. Let me still take away the harms I fear, not fear still to be taken. I know his heart.

Her sister's boyfriend was going away and he let Jane stay in his penthouse overlooking Central Park, alone, the way she or her sister couldn't be in her sister's apartment. The penthouse was two rooms sitting on a roof, like a doll's house with a panoramic view of the city. Jane walked into the apartment, shut the door behind her, and phoned Jimmy and asked him to come over. He said he was busy. She thought of calling Maria, but worried that Maria would think she's a sissy. Jimmy said we had to give up everything and quoted Meister Eckhart: "For verily thy comforts are thy foes."

He hadn't phoned the way he said he would. But it hadn't been that long. He must be busy. The play. Maria is a cynic. Her father left her mother when she was two and they weren't married and her mother was left with Maria and two other kids. Boys. Maria didn't like men, anyway. I bet I'm the first bastard you've ever met, she said to Jane. Jane smiled, remembering. It's better not to have slept with him. And two more weeks passed with his absence as felt as his presence. Jane wanted to tell Larry what had happened but didn't know how. Maybe she'd find him and kill him. Blood revenge. She didn't tell Jimmy.

Jane turned on the radio. "Sally, go round the roses. Roses they can't hurt you." Unless you press your finger on a thorn. She turned on the television and turned off the sound. She placed a book in her lap and watched the news turn into a commercial. "Sally baby cry, let your hair hang down." Jane looked at herself in the mirror over the couch. She couldn't read. "They won't tell your secret." The refrigerator was just a kiss away and she walked to it and opened the door. "saddest thing in the whole wide world. See your baby with another girl." At least she hadn't. Jane looked again in the mirror, then walked out onto the terrace. It was late. Jane felt old. There were views of indifferent buildings that looked solid. From other angles they looked flat, as if they were nothing but surfaces pretending to be more. Actors of a sort. Some people were still awake. Their lights were on. Maybe they'd fallen asleep with the TV on, maybe they were making love, or smoking a cigarette. Someone might be crying. Statistics let you know that anything is possible. A jet flew overhead. Someone is deceiving a husband, a wife. They're walked in on. The woman pulls the sheet to her naked breasts, the man grabs for his pants. Or a fight over money. Someone pulls a knife. Jane sees the scenes as set pieces with all the actors knowing their parts. Someone pulls a knife out of a kitchen drawer. Someone you would never think capable. A quiet boy. A good student. He never made trouble. Most murders, Jane had read, occur within the family or between people who know each other. A murder. A knife plunged into the naked woman's body, over and over, the way it would be reported in the paper the next morning, with her picture on page three. She's smiling. It's her high school graduation picture, the one she never wanted anyone to see. She put up a struggle and his skin is under her fingernails. Maria thought Jane was morbid. Jane told her it was just because she saw too many movies and read too many mysteries. One of the lights went off and Jane turned from the view.

Jimmy's mother was with him, but he didn't want Jane to know that. The lazy way out or the cowardly way. His mother would say that he lacked motivation. She had come to the city to bring him towels, new pants, and underwear. Don't buy me underwear anymore, he told her, his ass naked under his jeans. The flesh around her eyes quivered like Jell-O when you touch it with a spoon. He couldn't stand it. "I don't wear underwear," he said. And she asked, "Even in the winter?" Then, a moment later, "Don't your pants smell?" She made him laugh and his laughing made her laugh and suddenly it was easy to be with her. She even took off her jacket. Well, Kerouac loved his mother, and he was okay.

Alone, in this little house, safe, out of the world, isolated from it or so it seemed, Jane took off all her clothes and walked naked in the two rooms. She rarely was naked. In her family the girls covered up because of their father. Her sisters wore robes over their bras and underpants, everything taken off out of their father's sight. When she was little Jane wondered when she would have to cover up. Or stop going to the bathroom with him and watching him piss. Urinate, he said. Jane did stop doing it at a certain age. She covered up and didn't walk around naked anymore, but she can't remember when or how it happened. It came about naturally. Something must have happened. Something was said. Something that got lost. Jane stood in the middle of the living room, her arms crossed over her breasts. She might have been standing and talking to someone else, someone other than herself. When Jane was naked she felt that someone else was present, looking at her.

The King would speak with Cornwall; the dear father would with his daughter speak; commands their service.

Maria was saying that she didn't mean that Goneril and Regan were heroes, just that they had gotten a raw deal. And Cordelia was too good. But she disobeyed him, they didn't, Jane argued. But she disobeys and gets cut off from everything. Punished for her high principles. The other sisters get what they want. A kingdom to rule and power. Jane's coffee cake stuck to her fingers and she avoided Maria's eyes. "I'm going to title my paper 'On Being a Bastard,'" Maria said. "Or maybe I should call it 'The Firmament Tinkled On My Bastardizing.'" Maria's idea was that *King Lear* was about power and who gets it and why. You can lie to get it, kill for it, or be born to it. Whenever Maria mentioned power Jane felt sleepy.

He never wore a robe. He came to the breakfast table in his pajamas, loose and floppy, and he would hold the fly of the bottoms in his hand, to keep his penis from falling out. All of us never said a word and waited for it to happen. What would have been a terrible and expected accident. Part of our fate. She'd never see the actor naked. She'd never seen Jimmy naked. Felix had put his cock in her hand and said, This is for you, or something like that. He said that not too long ago when it sounded generous, and now it sounded like a lie. She supposed he didn't mean it, or meant it only for a moment, or only as an image that a poet might use. No one goes around pledging his penis, except poets and actors, she decided. She went to the refrigerator and ate some more. Maurice had been talking to Jimmy about Gertrude Stein and Jimmy thought Jane might like *The Autobiography of Alice B. Toklas* because it's like a diary and has a lot of food in it. Jane wondered if Gertrude Stein felt bad about being fat. Jimmy would laugh in her face for that. But just because she's a great writer doesn't mean she loved being fat. Jane had gained back all the weight she'd lost before she met the actor. Her thin period was how she referred to it, and Jimmy called it her blue period, after Picasso.

Jane fell asleep with the radio on next to her head. Rock and roll, the background to her dreams. The music was her first thought when she woke with a man lying on her back. It must be a friend, a joke. Jimmy trying to scare her like her father used to. "I need sex,'" the man said. "I need sex, I need sex, I need sex." Over and over. Jane twisted her head to look at him. He looked old. He looked young. He was white. Blond hair or bald. His penis was not hard, and even with her imperfect knowledge of sex, Jane understood that the longer the man didn't get hard, the more desperate he would grow, and the more time she had. "I need sex. Women don't understand," the man said. "I know," Jane answered. She thought about screaming. "Are you young or old?" he asked. "I'm young," "Are you a virgin?" "Yes," Jane lied. "Then I won't kill you." His hands tightened around her neck. The man pushed her head toward his penis and Jane resisted without thinking. He kept talking to her and she kept agreeing with whatever he said. His hands were around her neck again. She moved and spoke automatically, as if her behavior were willed or instinctual, an involuntary response for survival. He was shaking her, pushing her. Then he collapsed and began crying in her arms. The man said he had never done this before. Never. That he'd seen her through the windows. He asked her forgiveness. He said he was sorry. He said, "I'm going now," and got off the bed. "Don't call the police." Jane agreed to everything. "Give me time," he said. He walked to the other room. She heard the radio again. She lay on the bed and time passed. Another song. She heard the time, one-thirty, and thought, it's too early for something like this. He might be in the other room, waiting to see what she'd do, so she rose slowly and put on her robe and walked into the other dark room. He had gone or she couldn't see him. Jane called her sister, the one she lived with, and told her to sit down, that something bad had happened. Her sister said she'd be right there. Call a friend. Keep talking. Jane called Maria and woke her mother and talked with Maria until her sister arrived with the cops. Jane was lying on the bed in her flannel nightgown and robe. The police didn't believe her story. One cop said, "If you weren't raped, you'd be dead."

All three now marry in an instant.

Maria was rubbing Jane's back and singing a Spanish song to her. Jane said she thought the end of *King Lear* was the saddest thing, Cordelia dead, carried in by her father. Everyone dies except for Edgar. "Carried in like that, how I see it," Maria went on, "Cordelia's like a sacrifice. She may have been born into power, but she's not smart enough. She thinks that love's enough. And Shakespeare shows that it isn't." Love isn't enough, Jane repeated to herself.

Jane took the attack in stride. She almost accepted it. The lieutenant assigned to her case was a nice man who wanted her to make an identification. Pick someone out of a lineup. Jane said she would but couldn't make a positive identification because she'd never really seen his face clearly. She had no picture of him. Jane wanted to cooperate and go to a lineup and her sister worried that she was too cool about it. The morning after the attack, when Jane discovered bruises all over her body, her sister bought her French pastries and cried. Jane remembered looking at the skyline and imagining a woman being killed. She regretted walking naked around the apartment and never wanted to return there, the scene of the crime. The police said one of the window doors was ajar, the one she'd walked out of onto the terrace that night or the night before. She was careless. Jane wondered if bad thoughts had set the event into motion. She didn't speak about these ideas to anyone, except her diary.

Where does fear go when you don't feel anything? It was like Lois dying, all over again. Something happens and you try to find reasons for it. Finding reasons possessed Jane. Why he didn't call. Why that man didn't kill her. She felt sorry for him still and despised him. Evenings passed, the television on or the record player or the radio, and Jane watched or listened from very far away. She conducted dialogues in her mind with her sisters, her father, Jimmy, Maria. Jimmy was writing for a rock & roll band, and he was always frantic and exhausted. His response to the attack was to insist that they see as many movies as possible. Old ones. Like *Johnny Guitar*. It's so obvious, he said, loving it. He didn't want her to talk about it and she understood that. But not telling Uncle Larry was hard. Jane didn't want to see him cry or get upset the way she knew he would. Or maybe she wanted him to. Her parents were never to know.

Never Daddy. Daddy loves me so much he wants to cook me in the oven and eat me. Daddy throws me up in the air and always catches me. He pushes my swing and I don't get scared. He goes into a rage and screams and his face turns red. He takes me shopping and tells me I'm good. He buys me whatever I want and my mother doesn't. Maria had said it was funny that there weren't any mothers in *Lear* and Jane admitted that she hardly ever thought about her mother, to which Maria nodded and said she knew. Jane told Larry about the actor's not calling her as an explanation for not being in touch. Larry said, "There are other pleasures in life besides love and food." She said, "I never think about pleasure."

Chapter 14

When Emily left Edith's apartment for Europe, Edith stripped her room of things that were left behind and hung the painting Emily had given her on a wall that wasn't prominent. This time Edith thought she'd rent the room to a boy. For a change. Edith fought the idea that she, too, had been left behind, that Emily in her youth could just leave, almost heartlessly, her parents, Christine, whether or not the relationship was good for her. Could she have just left, announced to her children, Goodbye, this is it, I'm going to find out who I am or whatever people left for. It seemed like the plot for a situation comedy in which the mother would in the end be seen to have been only dreaming. And the feelings didn't last, because Edith hated sadness, and next to her husband's death, she could stand anything. Though sometimes, when the air smelled a certain way, suddenly she was in a different place, a street near her high school, and someone calling her name, Edith, from a distance, and maybe it was a friend, a boyfriend or her mother, long dead. Dead so long that saying it was like a date learned in history class. Only if she became the person she was when her mother was alive, if she conjured her up and became a teenager again, then Edith could remember the loss and it was palpable. Her mother could stand right in front of her and she could hear her voice. The best thing was not to think about it, not to breathe in that air, the air that's always sweet and light, the kind of air that holds memories.

Edith shook the rag in her hand and looked at the skinny mattress on Emily's bed, deciding to buy a new one. The mattress slipped easily off the bed; it hardly weighed anything.

Emily liked Amsterdam for all the usual reasons, but especially because she felt so removed from the city and its inhabitants. She was an alien and it was alien. "Foreign: alien in character, not connected or pertinent, occurring in an abnormal situation." She's not normal enough, she could hear her parents mutter to each other. Emily took a room in a house on the Centuurbaan that was owned by a woman in her fifties whose mother, in her eighties, lived with her, and always had. The house was large, with many rooms on each floor, and the mother and daughter each had a floor to themselves. They didn't get along.

What do you do with a feeling you don't want, Emily wrote in her notebook. Most of her feelings were unwanted. A letter intended for Christine was unfinished, one for Edith barely begun, and she'd written her own name and misspelled it, a funny thing to do for a proofreader, the only work Emily could find in Amsterdam, in a huge publishing company that produced English-language editions of medical texts. In German her job, she learned, was called corrector. The work brought her closer to Kafka, she thought, as she participated in every illness she proofread. The feeling was of being drawn to an older man with a wife and children. One child close to her age. It was obvious. It was something about his eyes. It was the way those eyes looked at her, as if they, or he, recognized her. Knew her already. It was a stupid attraction and she fell into it with longing and it kept her from writing letters; she kept on getting stuck at words like feel and fell being so much the same. She wanted to write to Christine and tell her, for at a distance Christine was an ideal friend, her best friend. Her feelings humiliated her, they were meant to embarrass her, and ever since she'd met him she couldn't shake the sense of its being fated, as in a fairy tale, fated and doomed. It was more than being in love, she considered that childish. It was written somewhere and she was inscribed in it. It didn't matter what she did, it couldn't be helped or stopped, and it wouldn't be. An immense sadness came over her that she knew was accounted for in the German language and not her own: It was different from depression, when you can't get out of your bed. It was like learning the difference between a city that's been occupied and one that never has been.

War on their soil, on their streets, the Dutch went about their business and cleaned the stoops and sidewalks in front of their neat houses, and no one would ever know from the outside what it was like. Being an occupied country obsessed Emily. One day an army walks in or marches in or shoots its way in and from that day to the next, lives are held hostage by an enemy. A real enemy, one that seeks to conquer and take over, not an imagined enemy, the psychic kind that Christine had become to Emily, someone who wanted to take her over, be her or not let her be. Love is like that, an occupation, being occupied by. He swept over me, she wrote, his body larger than mine, and I am helpless against him. I let myself be taken. Her own words unsettled her, marching in as they did from what, if she spoke it, might seem enemy territory. She couldn't tell anymore, she didn't speak it.

The aged mother, Anna, had been born in Vienna in its most exciting moment. Emily watched her frail, stooped body, bent almost in half, as Anna fed the cats that lived in their overgrown garden, a garden that Hilda might have loved for its chaos, and Emily for its naked symbolism. The wild cats were Anna's, and each day she descended two flights of stairs to call them to her with her thin voice. Her fingers were gnarled, Emily wrote in her notebook, never having seen such old hands, though gnarled looked wrong on the page, maybe because it was a cliché, and maybe twisted was better, a little different, but could fingers be twisted. She was barely able to set a plate on the ground in order to leave food for her wild cats. The daughter, Nina, complained to Emily about Anna over many glasses of red wine in a big kitchen. Nina had long red hair that she pushed back from her face as she talked. Sometimes she looked sideways at Emily, from behind her hair, holding it back from her face and posing, giving Emily her best side. Years ago she'd been compared with Garbo. And when she was seventeen the Nazis entered Holland and her father, a Communist, hung himself in their bathroom, just upstairs, rather than be captured. Nina and Anna went to jail. Those were the facts that spoke of lives about which Emily knew nothing and which Emily heard like a play or saw like a movie; the drama made it seem unbelievable as real life. People going to jail, a suicide for political reasons, a whole nation in enemy hands. It might have been a late-night movie with handsome men and women acting brave and noble, except Emily had never seen one about the Dutch resistance, and there Nina was, sitting across from her in profile, a face once young and beautiful, a living witness to something called history. Emily decided that history is what happens to other people, always distant and unreachable. In the movies noble emotions would have triumphed.

Edith didn't like her new tenant, a boy who was rarely at home and never lay on the bed with her as she watched TV and ate cookies.

She had her privacy again. She felt unencumbered and unwatched. A watched pot never boils, she thought. If she boiled, who would see her. Emily made her laugh, staying in bed all day long. She's not my daughter. They come, they go. The coffee cup was held in both hands, cradled tightly. She allowed that the sunlight on the floor was cheer 1, and that you could think something like that and be in a somber mood, and the sun did make her feel better. She didn't wonder that people who lived in Latin countries were happier, not wearing overcoats, not feeling cold. Maybe even in Texas. Poor but happy. Hoeing their land or whatever they did. Coffee from Colombia. Juan Valdez, the good life. The simple life. Nothing's simple, Edith said out loud in the direction of Emily's room.

Anna was struggling up the stairs, having fed the cats, while Nina and Emily sat in the kitchen drinking. The phone rang and Anna yelled that it was for the American because she sometimes forgot Emily's name. It was Emily's lover. He wasn't a boyfriend after all, and she'd have to call him something, and lover was right in Europe if wrong in New York. For all sorts of reasons, but Emily wouldn't think about that now, she'd think about tomorrow afternoon when they were to meet in the park. Emily didn't wonder where his wife was. Nina looked with interest at Emily and talked about her mother. "Anna knew everyone who was important in Vienna, *Fin de siècle*. You understand—the artists, the intellectuals, the philosophers, she would meet with them all, in cafés, salons." Nina paused to push her hair back and poured more wine into their glasses. "But you hardly tell me anything, and you don't have to, of course." This sentence functioned both as a digression and a progression, it could go either way, and Emily chose to let it hang there, until Nina returned to Anna and her life in Vienna. Anna, it transpired, was passionately in love with her Communist doctor husband, who was a bit of a philanderer. Anna passionate stooped cats twisted. The handsome doctor, an idealist, his devoted wife, occasionally betrayed. "There are many different kinds of betrayals and these tiny peccadilloes of men, it's not that much, is it?" Nina spoke as if to make a point, or so Emily took it, being in the position she found herself. Or as others might see her, even if she rejected that position. Her mother used to say position was everything in life. And now Anna can barely move, Emily kept thinking. Nina wondered what this American girl, so rich and young, was making of all this and whether she grasped any of it, and Nina kept drinking, feeling warmer toward Emily. "I had many beaux," Nina said, "the way you do now." Emily moved in her chair, wondering if she should go along with the lie or argue for her faithfulness. Anna summoned Nina, who left the room annoyed by the interruption. And returning, Nina said, "She's jealous of you, she's jealous of anyone who has anything to do with me. She says you take too much of my time." Emily wanted to run out of the kitchen. The drama now included her—she had become a character, against her will. Another position. Taken or given. Emily suggested that they all have dinner together. Nina said maybe, but it wouldn't be that easy, there was a lot of history between them.

Friday's dream: Christine and I are talking in a normal way. We're wearing winter clothes. I seem to be escaping from a big hotel or office building where I've worked and stolen some books. People help me escape but I can't get across a ravine and over a fence. I'm going to miss the train. Suddenly that problem disappears and I'm back in New York. Something about a lie bothers me. People think the words I'm speaking are my words, but they're not. He, she, him, her, anybody's words. I know I've stolen them too, like the books. Emily pulled the blanket over her head. He hadn't spent the night with her. He couldn't. Beneath her room was Nina's and Emily wondered what she'd heard.

Emily regularly appeared in Christine's dreams. Christine could have phoned her if Emily were in New York and not Amsterdam. Christine had bought Emily a thesaurus and would send it to her. Emily might regard it as promiscuous. They had discussed promiscuity before she left. "A miscellaneous mixture of things." It shouldn't have the awful connotations that it did, but it did. Emily asked her how it felt to be promiscuous and Christine got angry, that's really how the discussion got started. Christine got angry all over again. She said that it didn't really feel like anything. "Casual irregular behavior … indiscriminate." Promiscuous also means "not restricted to one class or sort of person." That sounded okay to both of them. That's why the lady is a tramp, Christine thought. Her new boyfriend had gone to his job, and later that day she would go to graduate school. Christine was determined to become a psychologist, if she could stand the people she had to train with. It was funny how certain conversations stayed with her or how she'd repeat them again and again in her mind.

The thesaurus arrived. Emily was despairing of losing her English and never learning Dutch. She didn't want to learn it. The thesaurus provided associations. One word could replace another but not fix it with meaning. There were shades of meaning. Things in the vicinity but not exactly the same. This inexactness corresponded to Emily's associations with the Dutch, who were very nice but incomprehensible nevertheless. But not to each other. Although when Christine or Edith or her parents popped up, almost like stand-up characters in a children's book, the possibility of comprehension fell down, and she knew it wasn't just language. But language—that is, having it—did help. She spoke English with everyone and English came back at her already translated. Emily took to saying that English was her mother tongue. She wrote that in a letter to her mother. Her mother received the letter and carried it with her to work, reassuring herself that Emily would return.

He reassured her as much as reading a familiar book. Each time she saw him she felt safe. When he placed his hand on her breast, she felt herself grow small, as if she could slide through her breast and his hand into him. He could do anything he wanted. She was his. It was simple. It seemed simple. She had never given herself to a man before, had never wanted to, had never felt very much of anything, and now her heart beat too fast, longing was an ache all over her, he could satisfy her, and she felt she would do anything for him. She didn't want to know about his wife or his family and he didn't press this information on her. She said she wanted nothing from him, and believed it.

Emily was writing more than she ever had. She found it easier to write at a distance, as if she weren't responsible for what came out of her. She finished the story about Christine, Keith, and herself. As she wrote she remembered screaming at Christine, "I can't do it," and Christine coming over to talk about it. Keith stopped his weekly visits. Her history professor was surprised that Emily expatriated, as she put it, because Emily was cautious, not taken by fantasies of adventure or possessed by wanderlust. Not being known is a big playground for any identity. Emily laughed to herself as she wandered around the city from one plaza to another, spending a long time at the flea market, watching the Dutch faces, feeling content with her foreignness and theirs. She was a tourist and a witness to her tourism, especially if she kept her notebook up to date as she planned. She had many plans for her writing. Detachment would keep her fresh, it was a kind of freedom. This sense of displacement. She would never have considered a married man before. She was being bad or maybe she was going crazy. Passion was a form of possession she wrote in her notebook, this bringing her back to the Salem witch trials, one of the last papers she wrote before graduation. Possession, according to the thesaurus, was occupation. Like love, like passion which takes you over and to which we are all slaves. I'm a witch, Emily wrote, briefly visualizing his wife and what that woman would do to her if she knew. If he told her.

Christine was reading at her desk. Emily had quickly answered her last letter. She seemed to think she was living in exile, judging from her letters. Emily was a literary romantic, Christine thought, full of Jane Austen and Kafka, though how she balanced the two was something she asked in her next letter. Emily replied that the more she thought, the more she thought things weren't one thing or the other but both. She could immerse herself in Austen's world then find herself in Kafka's. Then she wrote about her affair with Hans, the married man. It was against everything she believed. Christine answered that Emily might want to read *The Divided Self*, and told her about some research she found pertinent to Emily's situation and interests. "Infants move their arms and legs in time to the rhythms of human speech. Just moments after birth their eyes are alert and their heads turn in the direction of a voice. They prefer a female pitch.

Two grown-ups will stare at each other with the same intensity as mother and child only when extremely aroused emotionally or fierce enemies." Emily assumed this information was Christine's response to her having written that she and he got lost in each other's eyes and that she loved the sound of his voice.

Christine always felt uncertain after sending off a letter to Emily. She didn't know how she'd take it. She phoned Edith, who had also gotten a letter from Emily, and they compared notes. Edith said that if Emily were happy, she wouldn't be writing so many letters. Christine reminded Edith that Emily was a writer and that's what they liked to do. Edith still wasn't sure.

The television was on and Edith was watching it with a roving eye. Maybe Emily was happy. Or maybe she wasn't. But as Christine remarked, "Anyway, who's happy?" Edith thought, kids grow up too fast. The bomb, or whatever it was. It was the way it was now. Christine didn't seem to have any illusions. But Emily did, and that idea relieved Edith a little. Without hope life could be unbearable. But maybe that wasn't true. She didn't hope for too much. An old dame who's a little bit too comfortable in front of the television. Nothing wrong with that. Edith looked up, as if waiting for something to fall on her head, and when it didn't, and the commercial was over, she got absorbed in the movie she'd been watching before Christine's call.

Nina had drunk too much the night before and had heard Emily come in, late and alone. Her American tenant was charming, no doubt about that, but Nina didn't trust her. She was too young and yet not really naive. Nina put on her robe, avoiding the mirror at the foot of her bed, and went downstairs to see her mother. "Mama, why are you crying?" "You don't love me. You had friends here last night and I wasn't invited again. You never invite me." "Mama, you're wrong. I love you but I have to have a life of my own, my own friends. Please, let's not argue. Shall we have tea?" Anna grudgingly nodded her head and slowly engineered her body into an upright position, then brushed her hair back from her face, royally, the way Nina did.

There's a strange light in Amsterdam. There's no yellow in it, just a lighter grey behind dark grey clouds. It didn't seem real to Emily. Like Nina and Anna's fights. The three women were having tea together, and Emily was concerned to divide her attention evenly, while Anna was exhausted from crying, too tired to compete, and Nina kept things going with witty, nearly brittle conversation.

It didn't occur to Emily that Nina and Anna loved each other, even though they were unhappy and sometimes hated each other. Unhappiness had to be escaped from or denied. When Emily finished having tea with them and was back in her room getting dressed to go out, to escape, she felt that Nina didn't want her to leave, that she was deserting a sinking ship or betraying them by her happiness or eagerness to be elsewhere. The feeling reminded her of Christine, except this time she felt she was Christine deserting Emily, who was all alone at home. It surprised her to become Christine, it seemed too easy to be able to slip into one skin and out of another. She pretended to forget and concentrated on Hans. When she was with him other ideas were inconsequential.

She abandoned herself to this foreignness. Her passion was foreign too, and for it, for its truth, she could abandon lesser truths. She imagined that if, because of him, she could forget other people and problems, then there was a hierarchy, an order that she was falling into, that they fit into. Passion separated her from the world, it was her secret, a secret others knew but didn't talk about, and she carried it in her heart, feeling ruthless rather than romantic. Emily saw romance as sweet and pretty and what she felt was hard and difficult, almost a burden to guard and protect; it could be taken from her. She would have to conduct her life as if in a secret war with the ordinary world that always misunderstands someone else's passion. Passion and romance were different, she told herself, one was real, the other invented. Besides, she thought it would be good for her to be ruthless for a change.

Reading *Madame Bovary* gave all this credence. In the late grey afternoons she became all the characters at different times, passion being the book's subject. Rodolphe was horrible and cold but when he was with Madame Bovary he caught her fire, her heat. He could turn away but she could not. Emily thought Nina could have been Madame Bovary, married to a man she didn't love and whom she betrayed. Nina insisted too much that she loved her husband, and Emily pictured him like Monsieur Bovary, solid and dull, entirely devoted to his wife and despised by her. Reading this novel gave Emily the courage to go back and revise her story about Keith and Christine and herself and she ended it with paranoid fantasies taking over and the character Emily taking her leave of them and going to Amsterdam, where she meets a character not very different from Hans.

In a way the Hans character seemed as much a fiction as did her use of the paranoid fantasies, but Emily assumed it was because writing passion was writing the fantastic, sort of science fiction—which she hated—about love. With Nina sitting in front of her at the kitchen table, her reverie about love—fiction—was walked in on. Nina grabbed a wineglass and started talking. Emily made mental notes.

"When I was eighteen, after we got out of jail, the Nazi soldiers would flirt with me on the street and I would look at them with contempt, but was flattered that they noticed me and thought I was attractive and then I hated myself for that. Vanity is our downfall, don't you think?" And Nina's hands fluttered in front of her face, almost hiding it. For emphasis she would clasp one hand in the other. When she talked about the Nazis' desiring her she made that gesture. She said her husband had rescued her from men who were not as good or as respectable and had given her security and love. She didn't say this all in one piece but over the course of months of kitchen-table talk. And this afternoon she said that although he was good, he was difficult too and that men are like that, jealous of their beautiful wives.

When Emily left the house Nina imagined she'd fly into the arms of her lover. Nina's arms encircled her body, a reminder, and her wistfulness angered her. She threw her head into profile, as if she were being looked at and admired. She didn't miss love, she almost hated it. She only missed being a scandalous flirt, for the men at work with whom she did flirt probably thought it improper or undignified for a woman her age. She resented it. As if her sexuality had lines like her face, was weathered like her hands, had stretch marks like her hips. And was less than a young woman's, didn't measure up, couldn't satisfy, or worse, wasn't allowed to think about itself, to think about pleasure. You're too old for that. And there's carefree Emily, testing her womanhood. She doesn't know a thing. Anna called for Nina and the sound of that aged voice didn't seem to be coming from the outside. She wondered if she had called after all, and decided to ignore the voice until she heard it again.

There was no one between them to separate them, and their big house surrounded them, held them, and though they fought the battle was over. They couldn't live without each other. They survived together. Nina's mother insisted on life, would not give it up, and she was the barrier that kept death from Nina. That, too, was childish but Nina had stopped criticizing herself for being childish. Life itself was unreasonable, and she for one was determined not to try to make sense of it. Only fools do, she thought to herself as she finished the wine begun with Emily. Emily was a fool. Young and foolish. She laughed to herself again. Wisdom isn't comfort.

Emily wanted to abandon comfort, and had chosen to leave home so as to feel homeless. How far would she have to go to leave home? Could she bring herself back? And what would back mean? She indulged herself in a fantasy of orphanhood. She had been cast off, left to a fate that she by her own will must shape, grab as if from the air. But air is transparent, and she, she felt, was no visionary much as she had wished to have been a transcendentalist and escape the material world. I am escaping my parents' world, she wrote in her notebook. Maybe certain things ran in the blood. Margaret Fuller was related to Buckminster Fuller, his great-great-great-aunt someone had once told Emily, and Margaret had proclaimed, "I accept the universe." But Emily wasn't sure she wanted to accept anything.

She caught herself crying for no reason on the street. She couldn't pass another woman who was crying without pausing to look at that tear-stained face, wanting to know what was wrong, She read in one of the articles she proofread that crying had physiological benefits— the body wants to remove chemicals that build up as a result of stress. Tears prevent infection, one theory holds, by keeping the mucous membrane soft. She wondered if Hans ever cried and why. She supposed Nina cried a lot. She hated the way people's faces looked as they cried. Faces contort, crumple. They compress as if protecting themselves, pulling themselves in. The eyes shut tight. What we take as the person's personality seems to recede. People look as if they're being hit even when they're not being touched. There seemed to be something in this. You don't have to get hurt to feel hurt. The imagination is also physical. Everything is physical and mental. Like homelessness could be being out on the streets or just feeling that. When Emily cried she couldn't think, but she must be, she thought. People must be thinking all the time in some way. Christine wrote her that people also don't think they dream, but people do dream, otherwise they'd die. Why do people die if they don't dream. There again seemed to be a conjunction of physical and mental that Emily was fascinated by. She wanted to find reasons for her emotional life in her physical life, and vice versa. Some basic structures that would guide her or relieve her or allow her to do just what she wanted to do. If so she could be mindful and mindless at the same time. The phrase "words fail me" took on new meaning as she grew to distrust her thoughts, which were the same as her needs, she supposed. Words fail me. Words fail me. Words fail me, she wrote again and again in he notebook. Then, I fail words, I fail words, I fail words.

Emily and Nina sat in the kitchen, quietly talking so as not to disturb Anna, who, Nina said, can hear everything if she wants to. Anna's presence was overwhelming. Especially when she was absent, that small body loomed over them, vigilant, watching. But what, Emily wondered, was she waiting to see or discover. By comparison she thought her own relationship with her mother was not so bad, but she couldn't imagine living with her forever. That struck Emily as European. The old world that could be visited without being absorbed. Not a model. She watched Nina roll shag into a skinny cigarette that needed to be lit again and again, and fat already-rolled American cigarettes seemed to her representative of things that she as an American took for granted. And as one of the representatives of a powerful and dangerous nation, Emily was hard pressed to explain that she and it were not the same. Although as she sat at the table with Nina and watched her roll shag and listened to her stories about her mother, she found herself wanting to say, Find a place of your own. You can do it, it would be good for you. She recognized her Americanness in ideas like: things can change. Everything is possible. Just leave him. Her. You'll get the money somehow. Ideas about the frontier and a young country are unavoidable. Emily concentrated again on Nina's mouth, with the rolled cigarette stuck to her lipsticked lips. Her lipstick was smeared, and when Emily was sixteen she'd written a poem about smeared lipstick and her mother no longer wearing lipstick. She pictured her own mother, who rarely wore lipstick, sitting at the table with them, holding herself upright while Nina slouched. Wanton. Emily regretted the image and replaced it with Madame Bovary dropping her clothes at the sight of her lover. Aren't we all wanton, witches because of it. Nina threw one leg over the chair. She said very young men were frightened of her and all the other men she knew were married, only available for affairs, if that. As she drank, the skin on her face relaxed, her mouth loosened. Nina repeated that her husband had been a very, very good man but added this time that his being so much older had been a problem. Even so, she said they had a good marriage and never fought, or rarely. She said he sometimes disappeared into his room for a day. Then she stopped and clasped one hand in the other and seemed to be deliberating within herself and miles away. When she came back she said she hated him, despised him, and that he had hated her as well. She called him a bastard and said that on his deathbed he told her that he wanted her to be unhappy after he died and for all her life. He said he had never trusted her and that she was no better than a tramp. The awful thing was that she'd been faithful to him she said. Nina laughed, then cried, and suddenly was vomiting on the kitchen floor. Emily held her head the way her mother had held hers. Nina said he'd gotten his wish and Emily half-carried her upstairs to her bedroom and undressed her. The next day Nina apologized for her drunkenness and none of this was ever spoken of again.

In fact, Nina seemed to avoid Emily. And Emily felt more alien. She tried to think noble thoughts or to think about noble people, like Margaret Fuller, who died so dramatically, her boat sinking off the coast of Fire Island, drowning with her new husband, the Count Ossoli, and their baby. After two years in Italy, she was coming home from her self-imposed exile fighting for the revolution, at Garibaldi's side, metaphorically, no doubt. And now she was returning home to face everyone who had laughed at her, and she never got there. Never got home. There was something sad, even tragic, Emily thought, about how Margaret Fuller's happiness was not allowed into her mother country.

Chapter 15

Grace was listening to Lou Reed sing "I can't stand it anymore, more" when Mark phoned from New York. When he'd left Providence, Grace had taken him and his boyfriend to the train and waved good-bye as it pulled out of the station, Mark yelling, How often have you gotten to do this scene? And he grew smaller and smaller the further away he got. When he was no more than a blotch, Grace went to her waitressing job, cursing him for leaving until she got to the restaurant, where she stopped talking to herself because people think you're crazy if you do. Mark wanted her to join him and this call described the bounty she'd find were she to arrive. The pissoirs were more dangerous. One club made Oscar's look like kindergarten or maybe Lamston's. Every drag queen in the universe plus all the pop stars and fifteen-year-old hustlers who'd go home with you for a cup of coffee and a danish. Bliss, it was twisted bliss. He said his color slides were better than ever and he realized yet again what a terrible photographer he'd been, and he wanted to write a new play, something about Marilyn Monroe, and there'd be a role for her if she'd just get her act together.

Grace was thinking about studying acting, because even if she wasn't sure that she liked it, it was better than being a waitress. But maybe she'd change her mind about that too. Mark told her to read any biography she could find about Marilyn, just in case.

Show business was kind of appealing. Maggie said Grace might be an exhibitionist. Grace denied it. Maggie had moved into the room beneath her. She'd earned money doing almost everything, from being a short-order cook to being a call girl, the way she was now, once a week, which made it seem more like dating, the way she talked about it. She also did art, as she put it, and magic, concocting potions and drawing magic circles on the floor of her room, which Grace had to be careful not to step into or on. Maggie had one expensive dress for her dates, and that dress was good enough to go anywhere. The way she talked it sounded like the dress could go there without her, Grace told Mark. It had passed inspection by the madam, a woman Grace never saw but heard about. The dress was big enough to be worn no matter what size Maggie was. She could swell as much as twenty pound in two weeks, she swore, because of the moon and gravity and how she held on to liquid.

Black plastic bags of garbage lay strewn all over lower Manhattan and to Mark they looked like parts of a huge body that some maniac had cut up and scattered. People sometimes found babies in the garbage. He couldn't go for a walk without thoughts like that, even in a bucolic setting he'd wonder about what was really going on in the woods and behind the placid facade of a saltbox house. Mark was debating with himself whether sexual fidelity had any value at all, apart from staying out of VD clinics. Like anyone else his understanding of the present was tainted by some previous view. A moon landing looked fake or merely a reproduction of a fake. An original fake. Like me, he thought. The fact that moon landings happened even depressed him slightly, as if too organized or efficient, they left nothing to the imagination. But he doubted its existence as well, and finally decided it was part of that long list of déjà vus he'd stopped keeping. To think that when Oscar Wilde contemplated life after *Reading Gaol*, he expected there would be loveliness to look at. Mark jumped on an uptown train, to the Met, to look at paintings of the Madonna and Child because they made him feel peaceful.

Maggie's room was a mess but not as bad as Grace's, in which she could never find anything. Grace was looking for something she'd lost when her father called to say that her mother had had a heart attack. It didn't look good. Grace borrowed money from Maggie to return to New York, Maggie sympathetic even when Grace walked right in the middle of a magic circle, but Grace said she felt nothing. Maggie said it was shock.

Later Grace couldn't remember the order of things. The Greyhound bus skidding. The couple in front of her nearly fucking. Some guy who looked like a dirty old man. The hospital. Her father and brother. Did her brother say he'd never fight again unless they had landed on the beaches of Coney Island, and the nurse say that she could see her mother but just for a little while, then she saw her mother, who was all swollen, her face waxy like the bowl of fruit she kept on the kitchen table. Maybe he said it after she came out, to make her laugh, because she didn't think her brother was as much of a jerk after he'd said that. Her father crying. People she didn't know waiting. Grace hated waiting, especially in a hospital. Gave her the creeps, the nice nurses, the precious doctors. She told her father she'd wait somewhere else, although Grace felt her mother somehow knew that she was present, visiting.

Grace had nearly not been allowed into the transvestite club but Mark talked the doorman, who was a woman, although you'd never know it, into giving Grace permission. Mark couldn't believe that *Some Like It Hot* had been made in the fifties, even the end of the fifties. The first time he'd even been in front of transvestites was with his parents, a nightclub they'd taken him to, unaware, they claimed, of what was to come. There was a strip act done by one of the very best drag queens, not Lynne Carter but famous, and everyone was riveted on him. Her. Then came the big moments after all the bumps and grind and she, he, tore off the little top and there was nothing there. It was flat. "You should have seen the looks on the men's faces, men like my father. So disappointed. All this buildup and nothing." Mark couldn't remember how the women reacted because he was already so focused on men. "Born gay I guess," was how he put it. Grace looked around the club and thought she might be the only woman in it, although that was hard to tell, or she could say born woman, or was it natural woman or real woman. It didn't matter. She told Mark she felt like a transvestite.

Marilyn Monroe had at least four names, none of them her real father's. She had all her mother's married names, then her own married names, but for her acting name, Monroe, she took her grandmother's married name. Mark looked sadly into his vodka. She died thirty-five years to the day her grandmother was committed to a mental institution. Grace knew Marilyn's mother had been put away, but she didn't know about her grandmother. Talking about Marilyn's death made her think about Ruth's almost certain death, so she switched subjects, back to *The Misfits* and Marilyn Monroe's breasts. What a good comedienne she was. How she told people in high school that Clark Gable was her father and kept his picture on her bedroom wall. That *The Misfits* must have been a dream come true, because in it Gable loves her. Except he dies a week after the picture's over, and she thinks she caused it because she was difficult. "That's crazy," Grace objected loudly. It was almost a shout. Mark would later write a line for the play: "A silk scream in the night when it isn't quite right." It was too bad that Grace didn't look anything like Marilyn but maybe it didn't matter. Makeup, Mark thought.

The thoughts that entered Grace's mind upon leaving the hospital had ranged from picking up anyone to killing herself or someone to laughing at how dumb everything was to cold-blooded matter of factness. She hated her mother anyway. But maybe she didn't hate her mother completely. What difference did it make now. Ruth wasn't a mother. All of which reminded Grace of Ellen's chants in the mental hospital: "My mother is the Rose of Sharon, my mother is lily white, my mother is the whore of Babylon. My mother is better than your mother." Then Ellen stuck her tongue out and wiggled her fingers at Grace, the way kids do.

Ruth didn't wake up. The doctor said she had three more heart attacks and there was nothing anyone could have done for her. And if she had lived she wouldn't have been the same because of the brain damage. Ruth used to say she wanted to go in her sleep. She didn't want to know she was dying. And she didn't want a fuss. No big funeral. No graveside eulogy by a man who didn't know her, especially since she didn't think there was a God for anyone to be addressing. Still, Grace's father said that she had told him it was up to them, to him, to do what he wanted. Ruth had been convinced she'd die before her husband, as did her mother before her father, and she had repeated often, "I just want it to be fast." Secretly Ruth prayed that if there were a heaven, her soul would find peace in that next world.

Mark read some parts of *De Profundis* aloud to Grace, because Wilde was the poet of suffering and because Mark thought he should do something. Grace insisted she wasn't suffering. Mark read on into the night, and it was distracting, especially when, after a few drinks— he called what they were doing a wake—he began marching back and forth through his railroad apartment declaiming and ranting. Upon finding the passage where Wilde complains that prison attire is so dreadful prisoners are condemned to be the zanies of style, Mark shouted, "We're all zanies of style, the zanies of style died for our sins." His new constellation of stars was Poe, Wilde, Marilyn, and Jane Bowles, whose life ended in a Spanish asylum. She died without knowing her name. To Mark that fate seemed especially terrible for a writer, but in Grace it produced the image of her mother, all swollen, who also didn't know her name. Not exactly didn't know it but couldn't speak it. And what good would it have done for her anyway to speak. Except maybe she could have said something. Dead is dead, as Ruth would say, and homilies rushed into Grace's mind and out her mouth, so that after saying one she wanted to slap her hand over that mouth, but even that gesture may have been borrowed or stolen from her mother. "I hated seeing her dead," Grace announced, as if Mark and she were discussing Ruth. "Although she looked almost alive, but not as alive as when she was in a coma. If she'd spoken I bet she would have found something to criticize. Fuck her."

Mark considered beginning the play by having a narrator speak in a singsong voice, as if it were a fairy tale, some of the facts about Marilyn's life: Once upon a time there was a little girl who didn't have a father. Her mother told the little girl that her father was alive and showed her a picture of him that looked just like Clark Gable. Then the little girl's mother, who can't take care of her—she puts the little girl into foster homes—retrieves her to try and be a real mother to her, but fails at the part and everything else, and from the age of ten or so the little girl has a mother who's institutionalized. Her real mother refuses to allow anyone else ever to adopt her. So the little girl grows up an orphan, no matter who cares for her. With her mother and grandmother certified insane, the little girl fears the onset of madness all her life, but to protect herself she tries to find love and makes herself into the most lovable star in the world, Marilyn Monroe.

It was winter and the ground was hard. Mark had wanted Grace to wear a veil but she said he could go in her place, wear a veil, and no one would know the difference. Grace had thoughts like, when does embalming stop working? If Ruth froze would she stay like that forever, but then the ground would get warm in spring, the big thaw, and she'd melt in her coffin and the worms would get her, the worms crawl in the worms crawl out, they eat your guts and spit them out. But how do the worms get through a solid coffin, are there worm-proof ones? Her body had seemed hollow, lying there in the funeral home with those creepy guys around and people saying sympathetic things. People told Grace, now you only have your memories, but she wasn't sure she wanted to remember or, if she did, what would she choose to remember. She'd have to pick and choose carefully, to construct something that hadn't existed anyway. She could almost hear Ruth saying life wasn't a pretty picture with only happy endings. Grace picked up some dirt and threw it on the coffin. She felt peculiarly free, because she was really alone. Although when saying that to herself, she caught herself and restated it as if giving a lecture to someone else. There's no difference now. A bad mother deserves a bad daughter she thought as she walked to meet Mark at a neighbor-hood bar they'd soon call home.

Mark thought of Marilyn's life as a kind of in-the-blood tragedy. Revenge in the blood, of the blood. Blood tells. Grace had called Maggie in Providence. She promised to visit after finishing some work, and Grace didn't know if she meant a john, a drawing, or a circle, but she didn't ask. Celia was going to get married any day and asked Grace to come to the Midwest for the wedding, Grace said she'd think about it, but wouldn't. She told Maggie that her new roommate, whom Mark had found for her, was so skinny it would make Maggie sick. Sarah had the bedroom and Grace slept on a convertible couch in the living room. Sarah was supposed to be okay because she kept irregular hours and kept to herself. Her entire career she'd been play-ing nothing but ingenues, and since she no longer was near being one, she starved herself so that she didn't have any curves and hardly any breasts. "Flat," Grace reported to Mark, "like that guy doing the strip." She should have been heavier, her body looked like it was dying for weight. Large bony hands that didn't look like any inge-nue's, or should she say virgin's. Sarah in fact led a nunlike life and didn't drink, smoke, or eat red meat. What she ate was mostly white, and it was eaten with piety. Mark told Grace that Marilyn was raised a Fundamentalist and then became a Christian Scientist. Funny or horrible when you think about how dependent she became on pills. She always had trouble sleeping. Always. Maybe she was afraid she'd die in her sleep. And she slept with her bra on. Mark loved the sad-ness of her life. He and Grace went to see a revival of *The Misfits* and sat through a whole day's performances. Sometimes Grace hated her, the way she parted her lips, ready to be hit or stroked like a puppy.

"She's a baby," Mark said, "she should be the child to some Madonna. If I could paint, I'd paint without perspective, like Giotto." "The baby can't be a girl," Grace answered, putting on her black coat.

Grace wore black most of the time and when she visited her father he remarked that she looked like a Greek widow. Or as if she were still in mourning. Grace thought her father was crazy, and wondered when he'd find a woman to take care of him the way Ruth did, a widow or a young woman. Wash his clothes, Cook. Clean. Or maybe he'd just hire someone to come in every once in a while but that wasn't like her father, or her family. Little things of Ruth's, her knicknacks, sat primly on cupboards and shelves, as if waiting to be animated. Her father seemed reluctant to put them away and hadn't touched Ruth's clothes, which should have meant he missed her, but to Grace it was something about habit and the loneliness you'd expect after anyone's death. She hated the apartment.

Grace's shared apartment was all right, nondescript. She didn't bring people home. She liked watching Sarah eat her wheat germ and yogurt. She was so serious, they didn't talk too much, both avoiding the possibility that they might not like each other. But one night Sarah started screaming, a nightmare about a cat's eating her kittens alive for which Grace liked Sarah better. You tell me your dream, I'll tell you mine. And with this bond between them, Grace felt sympathetic to Sarah, who kept losing parts to real ingenues. Except for the time she played a young nun who becomes pregnant by a priest and should have an abortion but kills herself instead. Grace was not sympathetic to Sarah's character the night she saw it. But she was offended for Sarah the actress when her final speech—before she puts the pills in her mouth—was violated by a man's unwrapping a piece of gum and crinkling the paper. Sarah's concentration impressed Grace, who decided to take a few acting classes with her, though Mark worried that she might lose some of her naturalness. Grace said that'd be fine.

As if she'd been coached by another kind of acting teacher, Grace had a fantasy or a dream and she wasn't sure she'd been asleep. She is talking with Marilyn Monroe in her bedroom. They begin to masturbate with a vibrator, but they're afraid someone will walk in on them. Grace says to Marilyn, 'If I'd been your friend, would you have committed suicide?'" Reciting this to Mark, who wanted as usual to find a way to use it, Grace was laughing, but Mark said he might commit suicide anyway, she slapped him a little harder than playfully. Mark said he felt the same way, that he could save her or that he wanted to. "I bet she didn't even like sex," Grace said. "And no one will ever know that, the mystery no one mentions." Mark put his hands in front of his face, very Vincent Price; he said she took that secret to her grave.

Secrets. Ruth had plenty of secrets. Grace's father alluded to incidents, family fights, fears, as if he were tying to produce a new Ruth, a different Ruth for Grace. Or maybe for himself. Or keep alive the old one. It turned out that Ruth had thrown out all Grace's dolls and toys, her school papers and compositions. She didn't want the clutter around.

Surrounded by the few things she hung on to after the move from Providence, some of it contained in a small closet, safe from Sarah's cleaning up, Grace stayed in bed as long as she could, listening to Patti Smith and trying not to listen to Sarah rehearse for another audition. She painted her toenails red, though no one would necessarily see them. The red on her toes was a little trick to make herself feel better.

She'd have to leave soon to go to her new job. Working behind the bar for a change.

It wasn't so bad, except for the drunks. And now she was forced to hear stories as part of the job, which meant she couldn't just walk away if someone bored her. She had to smile. Or look sympathetic, depending on the story. Grace walked into the kitchen, where Sarah was eating her yogurt with wheat germ and a banana. At the table Grace and Sarah were a study in opposites, Sarah engulfed by a flannel robe so large as to make her feel even skinnier and Grace in her underpants and T-shirt. Sarah took small spoonfuls of the yogurt into her mouth and rolled her eyes upward, saying, "Isn't that good?" to Grace as if speaking to her cat, which she didn't have anymore, while Grace fixed a pot of coffee to get herself going, as if she were a car that just needed a push. The two had recently signed a lease for three years, and Grace said to Mark, "Now it's legal, I'm as good as married." But as Grace was leaving, Sarah started complaining about the dishes and the roaches and how Grace hadn't bought the milk in three days and as Grace didn't answer, Sarah's voice got louder and louder, Sarah maybe thinking that Grace hadn't heard and that's why she wasn't responding. Grace hated yelling. When anyone yelled at her she stood taller, looked right through them, and wished they'd drop dead right there and then, but she wouldn't show her anger, except to a lover or Mark. It was a point of pride, not to react, not to be the way they were, the way Ruth was. If there was a model in mind, it was one in opposition, although Grace wouldn't admit to thinking that much about it. Her. Every now and then she did wonder whether Ruth had a soul and where it would've gone and where it was right now. Did Ruth know she didn't miss her. Was Ruth hovering near her husband's bed late at night as he slept, keeping him from a second marriage. Or making invisible appearances in the scenes of Grace's life: the bars; when she said to Mark that Ruth could go fuck herself; when Grace was about to go home with someone, like that slightly older woman called Liz. Even though Mark said he hated his mother, he was superstitiously phoning her twice a month, and when his mother said things that made him sick, he told her he had to leave for the bookstore where he sold current fiction. He didn't tell Grace about the phone calls.

"Marilyn just wanted love," Mark was saying, slurring his words, looking as if he were about to cry. "A fifties girl or maybe a forties girl. Couldn't survive in the sixties, doesn't that make you sad?" Mark had discovered that in one of her acting classes with the actor Michael Chekhov she'd played Cordelia to his Lear. "That kills me. Doesn't it kill you?" "No," Grace said. "But can't you see her, the girl who never had a father, at Daddy Lear's knee?" Mark was pretty worked up, shouting that he hated retrospect because it was unfair to the dead. "Dead is dead," Grace muttered. You look at Marilyn and she looks like she could make you so happy. So soft. She looks like you could make her happy. But no one could make her happy. Everyone tried. She looks like she can give you everything, that you'd forget with her. But she can't forget, and she can't be satisfied.

By now the rest of the bar was caught up in the Marilyn myth, and one woman said that Marilyn had wanted children with Arthur Miller but miscarried and then couldn't have them. Mark, finding a comrade, walked over to the woman and threw his arm around her. "Is that biology is destiny in reverse?" Everyone agreed that life was hard, it was 4 A.M., bar-closing time, and Grace more or less carried Mark to a taxi, phoned his boyfriend and told him to be on the watch for him again. It was funny. She found it easier to talk about or read about Marilyn than to look at her, even though she could enjoy her films. Sometimes when she looked long enough, pity mixed with a kind of loathing, and a curious numbness came over Grace. She was fascinated.

Fascinated with her own fascination, Grace kept seeing all the horror films she could, especially the goriest ones. She'd even go alone. Poe would have been surprised, she was sure, at how gruesome they were, more disgusting all the time. But they weren't haunting the way his stories were. She wanted to be left haunted, to walk out feeling haunted. It had to be what couldn't be seen, wasn't defined or specific. A bad feeling that someone or something is never going to let you alone. Is never going to go away. If someone reported to Grace that at this place, this corner, in this apartment so and so got killed, she'd walk past that place and wonder if the murderer had returned to the scene of the crime the way they're supposed to, but more, did the murdered return? Did their souls rest? Or were they always watching, waiting to be avenged from the grave. The undead were vampires, but she was sure that the undead existed in other forms. People who refuse to die.

A guy came into the bar when Grace was working and ordered a draft beer. He looked like Ricky Nelson as a teenager. Beautiful purple eyes with long lashes, a loose wet lower lip. He said his name was John, and several drafts later launched into the story of how his mother used to send love letters to his principal, a minister at a prep school, and how his brother was an actor in Hollywood but was more interested in producing. John was carrying a roll of burlap that was meant to cover the walls of his apartment. That was the saddest thing, Grace thought, burlap. So later in the night she went home with him, and he made love with his eyes open, watching her face, her eyes. Grace said he should stop pretending and just let himself go. She told him what she liked, and he did it again and again, and walking home in the morning, Grace felt that leaden laziness in her body, but couldn't enjoy it too long because Sarah was sitting on Grace's couch, screaming about how worried she'd been and where was she and why hadn't she called. Grace told Sarah that she wasn't her mother and she didn't want another one, and when Grace told Mark about her new lovers, he said he was jealous. "But you have a boyfriend," Grace insisted. Mark admitted he was jealous of them, not her.

Grace's father wanted to visit Ruth's grave. To place flowers on it, with his children. To show respect, he said. You know what Oscar Wilde had on his grave in Paris, Mark said. "His mourners will be outcasts, for outcasts always mourn." Grace refused to go, saying she had to work. It was her brother who accompanied their father to the cemetery. Behind the bar, she carried on a silent dialogue with Ruth, playing both daughter and mother with an accuracy only she knew. Grace accused Ruth, defended herself, listened to what Ruth would have said in response, defended herself again, cursed her, provided other answers, remembered some things that softened her to her, remembered things that hardened her to her. She never expected to forgive her. And respect, that made her sick. You want to be respected, don't you? You want to be a nice girl, don't you? Grace looked at Mark and handed him a drink he hadn't ordered and said, "Fuck respect. She didn't give me anything."

John was beautifully unhappy, a lost soul like Montgomery Clift in *The Misfits*, which endeared him to Mark finally. He wasn't a cowboy, but had enough of the West in him to please an Easterner like Grace, though there was something frail about him, as if he thought he didn't have the right to be alive. He didn't make demands or requests or anything. He was just around, the way many people were in Grace's life. The connections were fragile, short-lived. People moved in and out and Grace said she never missed anyone. Every once in a while she phoned Maggie and said she might move back to Providence, but she didn't and she didn't visit as she kept promising. Maggie promised to come see Grace play Marilyn, for which Grace allowed her hair to be bleached blond, but Maggie didn't keep her promise either. Grace recalled a conversation she'd had with Maggie—it was easier to remember the stories than the faces—back in Providence, about how Jackie Curtis had stopped dressing in drag because it was harder being a woman. They laughed until tears came to Grace's eyes. Mark hardly ever wore dresses anymore, even at home. That time had passed. He told Grace he'd rather just be effeminate.

Lynne Tillman (New York, NY) is the author of five novels, three collections of short stories, one collection of essays and two other nonfiction books. She collaborates often with artists and writes regularly on culture, and her fiction is anthologized widely. Her novels include *American Genius, A Comedy* (2006), *No Lease on Life* (1998) which was a *New York Times* Notable Book of 1998 and a finalist for the National Book Critics Circle Award, *Cast in Doubt* (1992), *Motion Sickness* (1991), and *Haunted Houses* (1987). *The Broad Picture* (1997) collected Tillman's essays, which were published in literary and art periodicals. She is the Fiction Editor at *Fence* Magazine, Professor and Writer-in-Residence in the Department of English at the University at Albany, and a recent recipient of a Guggenheim Fellowship.

Self by Lynne Tillman, using Blackberry

Dear Reader,

This is a Red Lemonade book, also available in all reasonably possible formats—limited artisan-produced editions, in trade paperback editions, and in all current digital editions, as well as online at the Red Lemonade publishing community.

A word about this community. Over my years in publishing, I learned that a publisher is the sum of all its constituent parts: yes and above all the writers, and yes, the staff, but also all the people who read our books, talk about our books, support our authors, and those who want to be one of our authors themselves.

So I started a company called Cursor, designed to make these constituent parts fit better together, into a proper community where, finally, we could be greater than the sum of the parts. The Red Lemonade publishing community is the first of these and there will be more to come—for the current roster of communities, see the Cursor website.

For more on how to participate in the Red Lemonade publishing community, including the opportunity to share your thoughts about this book, read what others have to say about it, and share your own manuscripts with fellow writers, readers, and the Red Lemonade editors, go to the Red Lemonade website.

Also, we want you to know that these sites aren't just for you to find out more about what we do, they're places where you can tell us what you do, what you want, and to tell us how we can help you. Only then can we really have a publishing community be greater than the sum of its parts.

Finally, the publishing credits for this title.

This book was originally published by Poseidon, a Simon & Schuster imprint, in 1987. It was edited by Ann Pattie.

It was reissued by Serpents Tail in 1995, where Pete Ayrton was the Publisher.

Jeffrey Yozwiak, Cursor's first intern, OCR scanned it from the Serpents Tail edition.

Kate Gavriel typeset it to Fogelson + Lublin's design.

Lindsay Dodge proofread it.

All the best,
Richard Nash
Publisher

If you enjoyed *Haunted Houses* may we recommend other books by Lynne Tillman?

Motion Sickness

For the narrator of *Motion Sickness*, life is an unguided tour. Adrift in Europe, she improvises a life and a self. In London, she's befriended by an expatriate American Buddhist and her mysterious husband, or may or may not be stalking her. In Paris, she shacks up with Arlette, an art historian obsessed with Velazquez's painting "Las Meinas." In Amsterdam, she teams up with a Belgian friend, who is studying prostitutes, and she tours Italy with deeply mismatched English brothers. And, as with an epic journey, the true trajectory is inwards, ever inwards, into her own dreams and desires...

"A close reading [of Tillman] yields just how much her characters do want to connect, while preserving the right to their own process of intellection, the life of the mind. *Haunted Houses*, *Motion Sickness* and *Absence Makes the Heart* are nothing if not testaments to the belief that presenting the quality of one's mind in public is a means of connecting to others beside the self. In scenes of degradation, annihilation or joy, she contends with the idea that one's thoughts and gestures, while seemingly at odds, are married...attempts to accept the other not as a mirror but as a self."

— Hilton Als, *Voice Literary Supplement*, Best Books of 1991

"Literature is a quirky thing and just when you start to believe it actually has been used up, along comes a writer, Lynne Tillman, whose work is so striking and original it transforms the way you see the world, the way you think about and interact with your surroundings…"
— *Los Angeles Reader*

"A firsthand account of one woman's European journey and a riveting investigation of the troublesome notion of 'national identity,' *Motion Sickness* has true intellectual originality, a gorgeously sly dry irony, and a rich cast of thinkers and drinkers and eccentrics and hoods."
— Patrick McGrath

"This is Jack Kerouac's *On the Road* rewritten by the opposite sex in the form of vignettes of far-flung places and implausible encounters … Impressions, associations, and bits of conversation jotted during lulls in a mostly manic itinerary, coalesce into a densely descriptive narrative. The result is a keen portrayal of the postmodern world&hellip."
— Ginger Danto, *Entertainment Weekly*

"An intense and personal narrative. People and events are approached obliquely and never fully explained, as if we might know them already. This lean book is a welcome change after the baroque excesses of much contemporary fiction. Recommended for sophisticated readers."
— *Library Journal*

Cast in Doubt

While the tumultuous 1970s rock the world around them, a collection of aging expatriates linger in a quiet town on the island of Crete, where they have escaped their pasts and their present. Among them is Horace, a gay American writer who fears he has finally reached old age. Friends only frustrate him, and his youthful Greek lover provides little satisfaction. Idling his time away with alcohol and working on a novel that he will never finish, Horace feels closer than ever to his own sorry end.

That is, until a young, enigmatic American woman named Helen joins his crowd of outsiders. In Helen, Horace discovers someone brilliant, beautiful, and stubbornly mysterious—in short, she becomes his absolute obsession.

But as Horace knows, people have a way of preserving their secrets even as they try to forget them. Soon, Helen's past begins to follow her to Crete. A suicidal ex-lover appears without warning; whispers of her long-dead sister surface in local gossip; and signs of ancient Gypsy rituals come to the fore. Helen vanishes. Deep down, Horace knows that he must find her before he can find any peace within himself.

"Clever, witty, passionately written... Lynne Tillman writes with such elan, such spirited delight and comic intelligence that it is difficult to take anything but pleasure. ..."
— Douglas Glover, *Washington Post Book World*

"With *Cast in Doubt*, Lynne Tillman achieves several different kinds of miracles. She moves into the skin of a sixtyish male homosexual novelist so effortlessly that the reader immediately loses sight of the illusion and accepts the narrator as a real person. Alongside the narrator we move into the gossipy, enclosed world of English and American artists and madmen living in Crete, and at every step, as the play of consciousness suggests, alerts, and alters, are made aware of a terrible chaos that seems only just out of sight. But what impresses me most about *Cast in Doubt* is the great and powerful subtlety with which it peers out of itself—Tillman's intelligence and sophistication have led her toward a quality I can only call grace. Like Stein, Ashbery, and James, this book could be read over and over, each time with deepening delight and appreciation."

— Peter Straub

"Tingly, crisp, and wry. ...Delightfully clever and probing."

— Donna Seaman, *Booklist*

"Tillman's evocation of Horace and his life among ruins both geographic and aesthetic is a tour de force. *Cast in Doubt* recasts every genre it touches-the expatriate novel, the mystery, the novel of ideas-like a multiply haunted house of both form and identity."

— *Voice Literary Supplement*, Best Books of 1992

"A private eye in the public sphere, [Tillman] refuses no assignment and distils the finest wit, intelligence and hard evidence from some of the world's most transient artifacts and allegories. This is a truly memorable book."

— Andrew Ross

"If you can keep up with him, Horace will take you all kinds of places.... I was unwilling to close the cover and break the spell. I turned the book over and started over again."

— *Boston Phoenix*

No Lease on Life

The New York of Lynne Tillman's hilarious, audacious fourth novel is a boiling point of urban decay.

The East Village streets are overrun with crooked cops, drug addicts, pimps and prostitutes. Garbage piles up along the sidewalks amid the blaring soundtrack of car stereos. Confrontations are supercharged by the summer heat wave. This merciless noise has left Elizabeth Hall an insomniac. Junkies roam her building and overturn trashcans, but the mean-spirited landlord refuses to help clean or repair the decrepit conditions. Live-in boyfriend Roy is good-natured but too avoidant to soothe the sores of city life.

Though Elizabeth fights on for normalcy and sanity in this apathetic metropolis, violent fantasies threaten to push her over the edge. In vivid detail, she begins to imagine murders: those of the "morons" she despises, and, most obsessively, her own.

Frightening, hilarious, and wholly addictive, *No Lease on Life* is an avant-garde sucker-punch, a plea for humanity propelled by dark wit and unflinching honesty. Tillman's spare prose, frank, poignant and always illuminating, captures all the raving absurdity of a very bad day in America's toughest, hottest melting pot.

"Confirms and enhances her reputation as one of America's most challenging and adventurous writers."
— *Guardian*

"…should be awarded a special Pulitzer for the most perfect use of the word "moron" in the history of the American novel."
— Fran Lebowitz

"A book anyone concerned with urban life, women, or American culture, as it stumbles into the 21st century, must read."
— Sapphire

"Richly surreal ... yet darkly humorous ... Tillman demonstrates her wit, superb observational skill, realism of representation, and verbal eloquence ... No Lease on Life is a meditation on the realness and the ridiculousness of daily living. Yet again, Tillman tackles issues on her terms, freshly reshaping traditional literary forms."
— Donna Seaman, Booklist

"Exquisite... To encounter a writer of Tillman's acute intelligence writing as well as this is a cause for real celebration."
— Independent (UK)

"Tillman describes much of the wearing, wearying routine of the city's daily life—all that garbage, all those druggies and creeps and whores we've met in a million Letterman one-liners jammed into a scrawny crevice of land while the rest of America's so huge and airy and free. But Tillman's book is utopian precisely because it takes those things into account; because its heroine fantasizes about murdering all 'the morons' not out of hate, 'but dignity and a social space, a civil space, actually civilian space.' ... [Tillman] sprinkles the text with dozens and dozens of jokes ... Who can't relate? Isn't every public-transportation-riding, rent-paying, law-abiding urban dweller about two or three knock-knock jokes away from homicide?"
— Sarah Vowell, Salon

Someday This Will Be Funny

The stories in *Some Day This Will Be Funny* marry memory to moment in a union of narrative form as immaculate and imperfect as the characters damned to act them out on page. Lynne Tillman presides over the ceremony; Clarence Thomas, Marvin Gaye, and Madame Realism mingle at the reception. Narrators—by turn infamous and nameless—shift within their own skin, struggling to unknot reminiscence from reality while scenes rush into warm focus, then cool, twist, and snap in the breeze of shifting thought. Epistle, quotation, and haiku bounce between lyrical passages of lucid beauty, echoing the scattered, cycling arpeggio of Tillman's preferred subject: the unsettled mind. Collectively, these stories own a conscience shaped by oaths made and broken; by the skeleton silence and secrets of family; by love's shifting chartreuse. They traffic in the quiet images of personal history, each one a flickering sacrament in danger of being swallowed up by the lust and desperation of their possessor: a fistful of parking tickets shoved in the glove compartment, a little black book hidden from a wife in a safe-deposit box, a planter stuffed with flowers to keep out the cooing mourning doves. They are stories fashioned with candor and animated by fits of wordplay and invention—stories that affirm Tillman's unshakable talent for wedding the patterns and rituals of thought with the blushing immediacy of existence, defying genre and defining experimental short fiction.

"Lynne Tillman has always been a hero of mine—not because I 'admire' her writing, (although I do, very, very much), but because I

feel it. Imagine driving alone at night. You turn on the radio and hear a song that seems to say it all. That's how I feel..."
— Jonathan Safran Foer

"One of America's most challenging and adventurous writers."
— *Guardian*

"Like an acupuncturist, Lynne Tillman knows the precise points in which to sink her delicate probes. One of the biggest problems in composing fiction is understanding what to leave out; no one is more severe, more elegant, more shocking in her reticences than Tillman."
— Edmund White

"Anything I've read by Tillman I've devoured."
— Anne K. Yoder, *The Millions*

"If I needed to name a book that is maybe the most overlooked important piece of fiction in not only the oos, but in the last 50 years, [*American Genius, A Comedy*] might be the one. I could read this back to back to back for years."
— Blake Butler, *HTML Giant*